D0439581

PRAISE FOR LEE HARRIS AND HER CHRISTINE BENNETT MYSTERIES

"An excellent series."
—Pittsburgh Tribune-Review

"A not-to-miss series."
—Mystery Scene

"Harris's holiday series . . . a strong example of the suburban cozy."
—Ellery Queen's Mystery Magazine

"Another wonderful Christine Bennett mystery."
—MLB News

By Lee Harris
Published by Fawcett Books:

THE GOOD FRIDAY MURDER
THE YOM KIPPUR MURDER
THE CHRISTENING DAY MURDER
THE ST. PATRICK'S DAY MURDER
THE CHRISTMAS NIGHT MURDER
THE THANKSGIVING DAY MURDER
THE PASSOVER MURDER
THE VALENTINE'S DAY MURDER
THE NEW YEAR'S EVE MURDER
THE LABOR DAY MURDER
THE FATHER'S DAY MURDER
THE MOTHER'S DAY MURDER
THE HAPPY BIRTHDAY MURDER

Books published by The Ballantine Publishing Group are available at quantity discounts on bulk purchases for premium, educational, fund-raising, and special sales use. For details, please call 1-800-733-3000.

Harris, Lee, 1935-
The April Fools' Day
murder /
c2001.
33305209704752
la 04/24/06

THE APRIL FOOLS' DAY MURDER

Lee Harris

FAWCETT BOOKS • NEW YORK
The Ballantine Publishing Group

Sale of this book without a front cover may be unauthorized. If this book is coverless, it may have been reported to the publisher as "unsold or destroyed" and neither the author nor the publisher may have received payment for it.

A Fawcett Book
Published by The Ballantine Publishing Group
Copyright © 2001 by Lee Harris

All rights reserved under International and Pan-American Copyright Conventions. Published in the United States by The Ballantine Publishing Group, a division of Random House, Inc., New York, and simultaneously in Canada by Random House of Canada Limited, Toronto.

Fawcett and colophon are trademarks of Random House, Inc.

www.ballantinebooks.com

Library of Congress Catalog Card Number: 00-108954

ISBN 0-449-00701-4

Manufactured in the United States of America

First Edition: March 2001

OPM 10 9 8 7 6 5 4 3

In memory of Sister Redempta McConnell,
a wonderful person it was a privilege to know.

The author wishes to thank Ana M. Soler
and James L. V. Wegman for their
usual help and support. I count on it but
I never take it for granted.

And a very special thanks to
Carole Anne Nelson
for the title.

As much a fool as he was, he loved money, and knew how to keep it when he had it, and was wise enough to keep his own counsel.

—CERVANTES
Don Quixote

1

It was a particularly unpleasant March. It blew in like a lion and showed no signs of blowing out any other way. The trees and spring flowers that normally began blooming toward the end of the month remained bare. I cut several long branches of forsythia from the bushes in our backyard and put them in water in our living room and family room to force the flowers, checking daily for a hint of yellow.

Eddie, who had turned three the previous November, had one cold after another, several of which I caught myself, and even Jack, who was rarely under the weather, came down with a debilitating flu at the end of February that kept him home for a few days at the beginning of March. A windstorm in the middle of the month brought down an old tree at the far end of our backyard, narrowly missing our garage. Observing the damage the next morning, I felt utterly drained. It would be a big job to cut it into pieces the right size for firewood or for the DPW to pick up at the curb.

"I have had enough!" I said out loud to the cold air, the cloudy sky, and the still hard ground. But no one heard me.

Eddie had been attending nursery school two mornings a week, probably the source of all the sniffles in the family, but during March he missed almost as many sessions as he went to. That meant I had to ask Elsie Rivers, my chief baby-sitter and surrogate grandmother, to come to our house while I taught my poetry course on Tuesday mornings.

All in all, it wasn't the best month of my life, and I had T. S. Eliot's cruelest month to look forward to when March was over. Sometimes you just can't win.

It was in March that I ran into an Oakwood man I had heard of but never met, and I lived to regret that run-in. For run-in was what it was. I was in Prince's, the upscale supermarket—we have two in our area, one ordinary, one carrying more exotic, and more expensive, items that I like to buy for treats. No chance this penny-pincher will ever take something off a shelf that costs ten cents more than I can pay in another place close to home.

Jack, my lawyer-cop husband who is a fabulous cook, had asked me to pick up some oil-cured olives for a dish he was planning to make over the weekend, and I was staring at cans and jars of green, black, and dark red olives when I heard the sound of a small boy imitating a train or a race car. I wasn't sure which, and I looked down to find my cart of groceries gone and my son zipping down the aisle pushing the cart at a dangerous level of speed.

"Eddie, stop!" I called as I took off after him, holding a jar of what might be the olives I needed to buy.

But I was too late to avoid disaster. I heard a male voice say, "Ow!" and then, a second or two later as I scampered on the scene, "What the hell do you think you're doing?"

Eddie had managed to smack the man in the rear, probably rather painfully, and my son now stood looking up at me, his hands behind his back as though the cart had simply taken off by itself, and a sympathetic onlooker, of which there were none, might generously conclude that he was in the process of stopping it when its victim got in the way.

"I'm terribly sorry," I said to the man, who looked enraged enough to do us both in. "Eddie, you are not to push the cart by yourself."

He fought back tears, which had no effect on either me or the man rubbing the back of his leg.

"If you can't control that kid, leave him home when you shop. He's a goddamn menace."

"I'm very sorry," I said again.

"Sorry doesn't cut it." He then bent down and, to my utter chagrin, picked up a cane that had apparently been knocked out of his hand when the cart hit him.

I felt terrible. "I hope you're all right," I said lamely, taking Eddie's hand so he could not get away, not that he wanted to. "Can I help you? Is there anything I can do?"

"Keep that kid away from me," the man growled, taking hold of his cart and pushing it away from us.

"Eddie, you hurt that man," I said, lifting him and setting him in the child's seat, where he should have been in the first place.

"No."

"Yes, you did. You pushed the cart right into him and you hurt him."

"No!" he shouted.

"Keep quiet. We'll talk about it when we get home. I just need a few more things."

"You picked the wrong guy," a woman's voice said beside me.

"What do you mean?" I turned to see a woman that I knew vaguely from church, or maybe the town council.

"He growls if you pat him on the head. You're lucky he just walked away."

"Who is he?"

"That's Willard Platt."

"I've heard the name."

"He and his wife live over in Oakwood on the hill, a big house set way back from the road."

I knew the one she meant. My aunt had pointed it out many years ago when I was still a nun and came to visit monthly. It was a beautiful home, although somewhat forbidding in its setting, larger than I could ever imagine living in myself and, frankly, not the kind of place I would send my child to trick or treat on Halloween. "Well, my son has left him black and blue. I notice he walks with a cane. I really feel terrible."

"He probably won't do anything, but he's initiated some pesty lawsuits."

"That's all I need," I said.

"Have a nice day," the woman said breezily and went down toward the other end of the aisle.

I finished my shopping, got in the express line, and checked out. It was late in the afternoon and cold. I pulled Eddie's hood over his head and tied the cord. He was very docile, sensing my anger. I pushed the cart through the automatic door and turned toward where I had parked my car. As I crossed the car lane that ran in front of the store, I saw someone standing next to a car parked about twenty feet from us. I stopped and looked. It was Willard Platt, cane in hand, watching us. My heart pounding, I went to our car, which was quite close, got Eddie in his car seat and the bag of groceries in the front seat, and went around to my side. I glanced at Platt just before I sat down. I couldn't be certain, but I thought he was writing something down.

Although I am approaching my mid-thirties, lawsuits and upscale supermarket shopping and children have entered my life only in the last few years. At the age of fifteen I went to live at St. Stephen's Convent on the Hudson River north of New York's northern suburbs, and it was my home for fifteen years. I was a nun for many of those years, released from my vows and leaving at the age of thirty to live a secular life in the house I inherited from my Aunt Margaret. The house is now expanded, both in additions and in family, and my own life is very different from those years as a nun, years that I cherish. I am a suburban homeowner, part-time teacher, and full-time wife and mother, all things that bring pleasure to my life, except when they entail collisions at Prince's.

"It was my fault," I told Jack when we were having dinner later on. Eddie had eaten, taken a bath, and gone to bed. I had let him know I was angry and that he'd hurt someone and that I never wanted him to do that again. "I let him run around, I took my eyes off him—" I shook my head. "I hope that man wasn't hurt."

"You handled it as best you could, Chris. Eddie knows he shouldn't have done it. Don't beat yourself up."

"Does the name Willard Platt mean anything to you?"

"Platt? I don't think so."

"You know the big house up on the hill? The one set way back from the road? Probably dates back to the Fifties."

"Sure. It's not far from Vitale's Nursery, where we bought the annuals last spring."

"That's the one. He and his wife live there."

"Oh, that guy. I think he has a permanent gripe against humanity."

"What have you heard?"

"Well, he doesn't exactly eat little children for dinner but he's a general pain in the ass. Made it hard for the town when they wanted to upgrade the sewer over there and had to dig up part of the road. Insisted they post a tremendous bond and do some landscaping on his property that the town should never have paid for. Look, it takes all kinds."

"I expect he's in pain. He uses a cane—which our son knocked out of his hand—and when you're in pain, it's hard to be bright and smiley."

Jack gave me a look. "Relax," he said. "Knowing you, I bet you were nicer to him than anyone else has been for a long time. By the way, did you get those oil-cured olives for me?"

I laughed. Jack always knows what's important in life. "I did, and they were the cause of the trouble. I was looking over the olive shelf—did you know how many kinds of olives there are?—when Eddie took off with the cart. But I got the olives. What're you going to do with them?"

"It's a great-sounding dish: fresh tuna, pasta, those olives, and tomatoes. Maybe some capers in there—I don't remember. I can't wait for the weekend."

"It'll be here soon enough. I'll be glad to see the last of March."

As it happened, the last of March was Friday. It snowed in the morning and the wind blew so hard that small drifts formed on the lawns. They were rather pretty, very smooth, almost like sculptures, starting from nothing and rising in little hills, showing the direction of the wind. But as aesthetically pleasing as they were, I longed for warmer weather and less wind.

I was doing some word processing for my friend Arnold Gold, the lawyer, and happily Eddie took a good nap after lunch. He had become occasionally irritable about naps lately, thinking he was missing something while he slept, and I knew these quiet afternoons would run their course in the next year or sooner. I was able to finish a major section of my work before I heard him stir, so I closed down my work and looked in his room. He had been sleeping in a bed since his third birthday, a metal rail protecting him on one side, the wall on the other.

"Want to go out?" I asked as I helped him out of the bed.

"OK."

"I want to buy some peat pots for my seedlings," I said.

"Peep pots?" he asked, sounding confused.

"Peat pots. They're little pots for my tomato and pepper plants."

"OK."

He put his shoes on and I tied the laces. Then we bundled up and went out to the car. I drove to the nursery that was near the Platt house and picked up a bunch of peat pots and some good potting soil. I was a little ahead of myself, having just planted the seeds on St. Patrick's Day. The delicate seedlings were barely up and hadn't formed any true leaves yet, but I wanted the pots handy for when I needed them. Eddie behaved admirably, helping to carry some of the small packages I accumulated. The woman who checked me out gave him a lollipop, so he was in a fine mood as we went out to the car.

The nursery was on a hill, starting near Oakwood Avenue at the bottom and going up the slope from there. They stocked some wonderful things, and I knew if I was ever left there with a lot of money, I would have no trouble spending it. I'd had my eye on a beautiful Japanese split-leaf maple that just dazzled me. The entrance to the nursery was at the highest point, where there was a kind of plateau on which the shop and the parking lot had been built. I drove out the exit lane and then, on a lark, turned up the hill instead of down. In a moment we were driving by the Platt house.

I slowed down to a stop. "Look at that big house, Eddie."

He peered out the window. One house was just the same as all the others to him.

I drove up to the end of the road, turned in the little cul-de-sac, and started down. The plantings on the Platt property were striking, as were the trees. They showed more thought and care than we had used on our own piece of land. No one was about, and I sat for a moment, just looking, until Eddie called from the backseat. "I wanna go home."

"OK, we're on our way."

I turned the heat up when we got home, and Eddie and I put the peat pots and soil in the broom closet. Then we inspected my seedlings. They didn't look like much but they held a lot of promise, and that, I thought philosophically, was what life was all about.

2

On Saturday morning I awoke to find Jack's side of the bed empty, which didn't surprise me. He was a pretty early riser and he enjoyed giving Eddie breakfast on weekend mornings and then fixing something for the two of us.

I went downstairs and into the kitchen. No one was there. I looked into the large family room we built onto the back of the house, but no one was there either.

"Jack?" I called. "Eddie?"

No answer. No one was in the living room or dining room, so I went back upstairs and looked in Eddie's room. It was empty. So was the room we used as a study. As I was inspecting those rooms, I thought I heard a sound and I called again, but there was no answer. I glanced in our bedroom but no one was there. Feeling as though there was something I was missing, I went downstairs again. This time, although no one was in the kitchen, there was a box on the table. It was tied with a large pink bow.

"Am I supposed to open this?" I asked the empty kitchen.

No answer.

"Then I will."

I pulled off the ribbon, lifted the lid, and started feeling my way through the tissue paper. I took out piece after piece, but found nothing. Finally, I pulled out the last piece on the bottom and there, written on the bottom of the box in thick red letters, were the words: APRIL FOOL!

"Oh," I said. "You guys are too much. Where are you?"

At that moment, my husband and my son dashed out of the family room shouting "April Fool" at the top of their lungs.

"You two are really something. Where have you been hiding?"

"We tricked you," Eddie said, laughing gleefully.

"You sure did. I wish I'd thought of tricking you too."

"Admit it," Jack said. "This is one area we excel in. Don't even try to compete."

I didn't bother trying. I did a little thinking back to when I was a child and kind of remembered that my father had been a bit of a prankster. He had never given me a box empty except for tissue paper, but he had told me things that were unbelievable—which I almost believed since they came from my father—and then shouted the two magic words before I became too concerned. Although almost thirty years had passed since those days, it seemed I was still in the position of being the one surprised. Something to think about.

Jack and Eddie went out a little while later, as they often did on Saturdays, and I spent some time enjoying being home all by myself. There is something magical about being in a house alone. I love the silence, the feeling that no one has a claim on my attention and my time. I use those infrequent hours to good effect; I do the word processing for Arnold Gold, I read, I prepare for the course

I have been teaching at a local college. This morning I just tidied up, checked my seedlings, made sure my kitchen was stocked, and then sat down with the *Times*.

The guys were back by lunchtime, no surprise there, and Eddie decided to take a nap after he ate, having had a busy morning out with his father after playing a prank on his mother. I came downstairs after getting him into bed and found Jack working on the kitchen faucet, which had been dripping for the last week.

"I got a kit at the hardware store," he said. "I think this'll do it for a year or so."

"That's great. I thought I'd go back to the nursery and have a look at those Japanese split-leaf maples we talked about. I think they're awfully expensive but—"

"Don't write them off because of the price," my husband, who knows me well, cautioned. "Every time you see one, you say how great they are. I think we have just the place out front to put one, and I'd like to have it. See if they'll plant it for us. I don't feel too competent doing that kind of thing."

"OK. They have a bunch of them. I'll be back when I've made up my mind." And with that I took off.

I spent a very pleasant half hour or more, looking at various little trees, all of them still with bare branches. What Jack had said was true. I loved the curved shape of the branches and those spider leaves, especially the ones that turned red in the fall. And the front of the house would be perfect. They never grew very tall, instead spreading like an umbrella.

There were quite a number at the nursery, two of them very small, the others a little larger. Although the larger ones cost more, I decided it might be worth it to have a more mature tree, one that had survived more winters. I finally picked out the perfect one and talked to one of the men about having it planted. It was fine with him, but he wanted to wait till the ground was a little softer. We concluded our deal and I went back for a last look at my new tree. The nursery man had tied on a red and yellow SOLD tag, and I had a happy feeling of ownership as I walked back to the car.

It was still early in the afternoon, and as I drove out of the nursery, on a whim I turned right to go up the hill. The sun was shining, I owned a red Japanese split-leaf maple, and I thought it would be nice to look around, especially from a height. I drove up the hill slowly, looking to my left as I reached the Platt house. The driveway was empty, the garage doors down. The mailbox at the end of the drive had a red flag up. As I went by the lawn I saw something not far from the shrubbery near the house. I stopped the car and looked, but the sun was in my eyes.

Something was lying on the grass, not moving. I felt a touch of anxiety. I turned off the motor, grabbed the key, and got out of the car. It wasn't the kind of road where you had to check left and right before crossing; there were no cars above the nursery and no other houses after this one.

I ran across the lawn, feeling my anxiety turn to panic. Someone was lying there. I heard myself say "No" as I approached the still form. It was a man, probably Willard Platt, lying on his stomach. A cane lay out of reach of his right hand. But it was worse than that. The handle of a knife stuck out of the middle of his back. Someone had stabbed him to death.

3

For a moment I was frozen. I couldn't think. I didn't know what to do. I said, "Mr. Platt? Mr. Platt?"

The still form did not move. I ran to the door of the house and rang the bell and pounded on the door, calling, "Hello? Anyone home?"

It was as quiet inside as outside. I had to do something but my mind refused to function. I looked at the body one more time, then raced across the lawn to my car, started the motor, made a U-turn, and went down the hill. I was closer to my house than the police station so I drove home, my hands gripping the steering wheel. As I came to the end of the steep road, a van loaded with people turned into it, nearly colliding with me. My shoulders were shaking. I was muttering things to myself, that this could not be, it was not happening.

I stopped the car halfway up the driveway and dashed into the house calling, "Jack? Jack? Are you there?"

"I'm right here. What's up?" He came around the corner toward me and we collided. "Calm down, Chris. What's wrong?"

"There's a body. Jack, Mr. Platt is dead. He's been

stabbed. I just found him. He's lying on the ground in front of his house. No one's home. Call the police."

He said something under his breath, marched me into the kitchen and sat me down in a chair. Then he poured some juice from a container in the refrigerator, set it down in front of me and ordered me to drink. When I had, he said, "OK, now tell me this again."

I did, a little more slowly.

"You're sure he's dead?"

I nodded.

"With a knife in his back?"

"Yes. He was lying on his stomach. His cane was on the grass a foot or so away from the body."

He took the phone and called 911. As I tried to calm myself, I heard him tell the police essentially what I had told him.

"OK, fine. Yeah. And let me know what's up." He hung up and sat beside me. "You OK?"

I nodded. I had my hand against my chest. I swallowed and wiped the moisture from my eyes. I wasn't quite crying, but I wasn't not crying either. "I can't believe this," I said finally.

"What were you doing at his house?" Jack asked.

"I don't know." I tried to recall what had taken me there. "I went to the nursery and bought us a Japanese maple. Then I decided to drive up the hill, just to see the view. It was so nice out." I looked at him but his face gave away nothing. In the last seconds, he had become a cop. "I passed the Platt house and saw something lying on the grass. It was Willard Platt."

"You got out of the car?"

"Yes. I crossed the road and went over to see what was

wrong. There was a knife sticking out of his back. His cane—" A shudder ran through me. "It was lying on the ground near his right hand. That's all I remember. I banged on the door but no one was home. So I came here. Jack, I don't believe this is happening."

"I think I'll drive over there and see what's going on."

I wanted to tell him to stay, but I let him go. My panic had subsided a little. Maybe a cup of tea would calm me down further.

Jack put his jacket on and came back to the kitchen. He put his arm around me and gave me a squeeze. As he started for the door, the phone rang. I listened while he answered.

It was a strange conversation that made no sense to me, but when he hung up, he unzipped his jacket. "Willard Platt's OK," he said, taking the jacket off.

"What? Who just called?"

"One of the cops."

"If Platt's not dead, who did I just see at the Platts' house?"

"It was Platt, but he wasn't dead."

"I don't understand."

"There's apparently an annual treasure hunt going on. The drama club at the high school picked today for it since it's Saturday and it's April Fools' Day."

"That was an April Fools' joke?"

"Sort of. One of their clues led them to the Platts'. They were supposed to find a weapon of murder."

"But—"

"But it wasn't a real knife. It was a stage prop. If you'd touched it—which I know you wouldn't've—you would've seen that it was soft. It couldn't hurt anyone."

"The van," I said.

"What?"

"A van turned into the Platts' road as I got to the bottom of the hill. It must have been the drama students going up to their house."

"Could be. The cop said the police got there as the kids were leaving."

"I need a cup of tea."

"Make two. I'm not going anywhere."

I still didn't feel entirely steady on my feet but I put some water on to boil and got a tin of tea out of the cabinet. It was a nice English tea that my friend Melanie's mother had brought back from London for me. I stuck my nose in it for the aroma and somehow that calmed me down.

We sat at the kitchen table, sipping from our mugs. "I feel like a fool," I said.

"It wasn't your fault."

"I thought Willard Platt was supposed to be an unpleasant person. What possessed him to lie down on the grass in the cold and pretend to be dead?"

"You got me. Maybe there's a warm fuzzy side to him that I hadn't heard about."

"And why didn't he have the decency to let me know he was OK?"

"That's the cold hard side."

"Thank God he's all right. Jack, I hope you aren't planning any more surprises for me today."

"I promise, we did our thing this morning. If I'd known the way this day was going to turn out, I wouldn't have done it."

"I'm not blaming you. I just feel scared and confused. I never want anything like this to happen again."

"Don't worry. It won't."

I guess I'm still that gullible kid that my father played jokes on. I believed him.

It's the understatement of the year to say that I am not an accomplished cook. I'm so much better than I was when I left the convent at age thirty, that I sometimes think I'm better than I am. What I've done is learn, with the help of Jack and my friend Mel, to cook things that are fail-safe and that taste good besides. I can now roast a chicken whose wonderful scent permeates the house and gives me a couple of hours of olfactory pleasure before I dig in to appreciate the taste.

But it's Jack who really loves to cook, and I've made up my mind it's probably in the genes, as his sister runs a catering business with their mother, obviously an inherited talent. So on weekends I defer to his greater ability and skill and reserve my pleasure for eating. He clatters around more than I do, and I think he uses more pots and pans, but it's worth it. On that April first, I was just glad I didn't have a meal to cook.

When Eddie got up, we went out for a walk, ending up at the home of a neighbor who had recently moved in with a small boy almost exactly Eddie's age. I didn't tell Janet, the mother, what I had gone through earlier. Instead we put the two little boys together with a lot of toys and we talked about local politics and a little gossip.

After about an hour and a half I got Eddie to agree to go home and we left. I was feeling much better and even starting to think that I had overdone it. Maybe if I had touched Mr. Platt, I would have seen he was still alive. But I had been so scared and it was a crime scene. I shuddered as I thought about it.

Jack was organizing his ingredients for dinner when we got home, so Eddie and I set the table and then went into the family room to get out of Jack's way. I hadn't seen the paper yet and I was reading a story that involved the NYPD, a subject close to our hearts since it's not just Jack's employer but also a huge piece of his life, when the phone rang.

"I'll get it," I called, dropping the paper and making for the kitchen. "Hello?"

"Chris, it's Mel. Have you heard?"

"Heard what? Mel, if this is an April Fools' joke, I don't want to hear it."

"What happened? You don't sound your usual chipper self."

"I'm not my usual chipper self. It's been a tough April Fools' Day."

"Oh. Sorry. Well, this is no joke. There's been a murder in Oakwood."

I almost groaned. "Mel, there hasn't been a murder. It was an April Fools' Day prank, a treasure hunt or something. He's alive and well and I don't know how the story has gotten around. There's nothing to it."

There was silence. "I didn't even tell you who was murdered."

"No one was murdered. Believe me. It's just a bad joke."

"It's not a joke, Chris. He's dead."

"Who's dead?" I asked.

"Willard Platt, the man who lives over on the hill above the nursery."

I took a deep breath. "That's the murder that isn't a murder. I'm responsible for the uproar, in a way." I outlined what had happened, my trip to the nursery, my discovery of the apparently dead body, and then the repercussions. "So you see," I finished, "there's nothing to it. It was all some kind of joke and I got in the middle of it by accident and I really don't want this awful story spread any further."

Mel said nothing.

"Mel? Are you there?"

"I'm very confused."

"Well, there's nothing to be confused about. He's alive and well and was just cooperating with the high school drama club."

"I'll call you back." She hung up.

I put the phone back and looked at Jack, who had stopped working to see what was going on. "This terrible story is making the rounds," I said. "That was Mel. What possessed me to go to that nursery today? Why couldn't I have stayed home and read the paper?"

"Because you're not a stay-at-home person. I'm sorry this has gotten out of hand. I don't know who's spreading the story. Can't be the high school kids. From what the cop told me, it sounds like they just came, took what they were looking for, and left."

"Well it isn't me," I grumbled. "I'm not telling anyone." I took a carrot stick from the counter and started chewing as I went back to the family room.

I picked up the *Times* and found the article I had been reading, looked down the column till I located my place, and started reading again. Eddie came over and asked for a pretzel and we went back to the kitchen to fortify ourselves. I happen to like pretzels too, so I took one for myself.

When I got back into the *Times* once more, the phone rang. I jumped up, feeling surly, and walked past Jack to the phone. "Hello," I said in a less than pleasant voice.

"Chris?" It was Mel.

"Yes. Sorry. I'm feeling peeved."

"Chris, Willard Platt is dead. He was stabbed to death this afternoon—not very long ago—outside his house. One of the teachers was over at the police station a little while ago and heard about it. There's no question. He's dead."

I held the phone at my side for a moment, trying to think of what to say. Then I brought it back to my ear. "I'll call you back."

"You're not gonna tell me he's dead," Jack said.

"Please call the police, Jack. I just want this settled so I can put it behind me."

He rinsed his hands and dried them on a paper towel, took the phone and dialed. I listened while he identified himself and asked the question. There were a lot of uh-huhs and finally a thank-you. He hung up and looked me. "It's no joke. Platt was out working in his garage, according to his wife. This was after the high school kids and the police left. She called him in for something and he didn't answer, so she went to look. She found him dead on the ground outside the garage."

I felt close to tears. I had the sense of not knowing what was real and what was fantasy. I had found a body that was not a body and now the man was dead, probably having been murdered not far from where I'd seen him lying.

"Sit down," Jack said.

I sat at the kitchen table, aware that this was the second time today that I had lived through this scene.

"I don't know what to say," he said.

I shrugged and shook my head, swallowed to get rid of the lump. "This can't be happening."

"He wasn't kidding me."

"What is going on?"

"I don't know."

"I'd better call Mel. I think she thinks I'm losing my mind, probably because I am." I got up and dialed her number. It was busy. She was probably calling around to find out what was happening. I hung up.

"We need a cordless phone, Chris. We're the last Americans without one."

"Joseph doesn't have one." Sister Joseph is the General Superior of St. Stephen's Convent, my home as a nun. She is also the person in the world I feel closest to outside my immediate family.

"We do not live in a convent. Maybe I'll give them one as a gift next Christmas."

I smiled.

"Thank God you can smile. I thought you'd really gone to pieces."

"I am in pieces. The smile is a reflex. What does Joseph need a cordless phone for? She takes calls at her desk. I don't think she wants to walk around talking. She wouldn't have her notes in front of her. And don't even think of a cell phone. Women walk up and down the aisles of the supermarket now talking to their friends. And when they're driving, they forget to go on the green light because their conversations are so important."

Jack grinned. "Good. You haven't lost it. Glad your value system's still in place."

I poked him and tried Mel's number again.

"Hello?"

"It's Chris."

"Chris. Are you OK?"

"No, but I'm surviving. You're right and I'm right. Mr. Platt was apparently murdered sometime after I thought he was but he wasn't."

"Right. Do they know who did it?"

"If they do, they didn't tell Jack. He called the police and they usually answer him pretty fully. Professional confidences exchanged between police are a currency of the job." I sketched out what he had heard.

"This is very scary."

"I know."

"There's a killer in Oakwood. Hold on. I want to lock my kitchen door." I heard her open the door and slam it shut. "OK. I feel better. Not really, but you know."

I did know. "Look, Mel, I have to think. I'll call you later."

"Make it tomorrow. We're going out tonight. Except I wonder if I want to leave the kids with a sitter after this."

I wondered the same thing. "I'll talk to you tomorrow." I hung up. Then I checked the doors to the outside, making sure they were closed tightly and locked.

"We have a killer in town," I said to Jack, looking over my shoulder to make sure Eddie wasn't listening. "Mel's scared and I'm scared and I think all reasonable people should be scared."

"Stop being so damn reasonable. You're right. This is really a bad scene. We'll talk about this later."

4

The rest of the afternoon was crazy. The phone kept ringing with neighbors asking what we knew, since Jack always had a little more information than most of the other townspeople. The Platts lived in an area where they had no neighbors and there was little direct information, but everyone seemed to have heard that there was a murder. I ran back and forth from the family room to the kitchen so many times I was ready to run out and buy a cordless phone myself by the time we sat down to dinner.

The dinner, of course, was very good. Although Jack's fingernails were black from pulling apart the oil-cured olives to remove the pits, he agreed the dish was worth the trouble. We grated some fresh Parmesan over it—Jack won't let me buy the already grated stuff anymore; he says it isn't flavorful enough—and it was a great treat.

After Eddie was off to bed, I started thinking about tomorrow's breakfast and that's when I discovered I was out of milk. At the same time, Jack asked if we had anything sweet to go with our coffee?

It had been on my shopping list, which was totally forgotten after my discovery of Willard Platt's "body."

"I'll go and get something. I need milk anyway."

"I'll go. You stay home."

I looked at him, assessing the situation. "I'll feel better if I'm in a car and you're home with Eddie."

"Chris, I really don't think—"

"We don't know what's going on, Jack. The parking lot at Prince's is well-lighted. And I want you home."

"OK. Let me walk you out to the car."

That's when I knew that what he was saying and what he was thinking were two different things. I backed out of the driveway and went up to Oakwood Avenue. Where we live, it's a quiet, residential street, but farther along there are stores, including the supermarket I was aiming for. But not far from our street, I came to the road up to the nursery and the Platts' house. On a sudden whim, I turned right.

The nursery was closed for the night, a few lights on here and there to discourage unwanted visitors. I continued up the hill to the Platts'. There were lights on and yellow crime scene tape marking off the driveway and the garage. I sat for a moment, looking at the still house and grounds, wondering if Mrs. Platt had remained at home. After a couple of minutes, I made my U-turn and went back down the hill, turned onto Oakwood Avenue, and continued toward Prince's.

Oakwood Avenue is not well-lighted until you get into the center business area. At this point it was just one lane in each direction with a line down the center that alternately allowed this lane of traffic or that one to pass. Suddenly on my right I saw a dark figure walking just to the right of the road, hardly far enough away to be safe from a wide car or a truck. I slammed my brakes on, feeling the panic of having almost been involved in a terrible accident. The dark figure was just to my right and silhouetted in my headlight. I inched forward and wound down the window, remembering to put my emergency blinkers on so I would not get smacked from behind.

The figure turned and looked at me. It was a woman, an older woman. She looked almost lost.

"Can I help you?" I said. "Can I take you somewhere?"

"I'm just going to my son's house."

"Is it far?"

"It's just in the next town."

"The next town? Please get in. I'll drive you."

She hesitated, perhaps wondering, as I had, if it was safe to get in the car of a stranger. I guess I didn't look very forbidding as she pulled the door open and sat down beside me. "Thank you. That's very nice of you."

"I'm Chris Brooks," I said, using my married name, as in this milieu I would be known as Jack's wife.

"I'm Winnie Platt."

"Mrs. Platt!" I didn't know what to say. "Are you—are you Willard Platt's wife?"

"For forty-eight years," she said.

"I heard what happened. I'm terribly sorry."

"Thank you."

"Where is your son's house?" I asked, wondering why her son had not come to see her when he heard the news of his father's death.

"Just keep going. I'll show you where to turn."

I pulled onto the road and drove toward the center of town. "It's really dangerous to walk on Oakwood Avenue. Cars come by at forty miles an hour. You weren't very visible."

"I don't drive," she said. "I used to, but I haven't driven since the accident."

I let that be. "Are you all right, Mrs. Platt?"

"Yes."

"Could I stop and get you something to eat?"

"I'm not hungry. My daughter-in-law will have something if I need it."

I made a few turns at her direction and crossed over into the adjoining town. It had much the same character as Oakwood, and without a sign at the border, you wouldn't know you had traded in one mayor and council for another, one police department for another, one volunteer fire department for one just like it.

I had taken note of the mileage when I picked her up. Her little walk was over a mile and a half. I pulled into the driveway of a house larger and newer than ours. "Will you stay overnight?" I asked.

"I don't like to stay in other people's houses. I just want to talk to my son. He'll drive me home."

I got out of the car and went around to help her out. We walked to the front door together and she pushed the bell. A woman older than I opened the door and seemed stunned to see Mrs. Platt.

"Winnie," she said. Then she looked at me.

"I'm Chris Brooks. I found your mother-in-law walking on the road to come here. I thought it would be safer for her to go in a car."

"Please come in. I'm so sorry to put you out. I thought my husband had gone to get her. Give me your coat, Winnie, and sit down. I'll call Roger and see what's keeping him."

"He should have come," her mother-in-law said.

"I couldn't reach him."

Then you should have come, I thought. What is the matter with this family?

The younger Mrs. Platt did not introduce herself or offer to take my coat, but I followed the older woman to the living room and sat down beside her on the sofa, setting my coat on a chair. Her daughter-in-law returned from the coat closet in the large front hall and sat on a chair facing us. It was a beautiful room, with a thick carpet and draperies that showed a professional touch.

"Is your husband working?" I asked, wondering what could keep a man away when his father had been murdered.

"No, he's—well, yes, actually. He's involved in a very important project. Winnie, would you like a cup of tea? Are there any phone calls I can make for you?"

"I want to talk to Roger." Mrs. Platt took her pocketbook, which she had set on the floor near her feet, put it on her lap and opened it. She rummaged in it for a moment, then closed it and put it back on the floor. She was a woman of about seventy, give or take a couple of years, wearing no makeup, and dressed in a shapeless black dress with large black buttons down the front. She looked grandmotherly, but not particularly healthy. Her skin was sallow and she looked worn. "Did you call him, Doris?"

"Oh. No, I didn't. I'm sorry; it slipped my mind. Let me give him a ring." She jumped up as though she were happy to be leaving us, and disappeared. From another room I heard her voice.

She came back and said, "He's on his way. I got him in his car."

As I started to think that I was not needed here anymore,

the daughter-in-law said, "Is there anything I can do for you, Mrs. Brooks?"

"Thank you, I think I'll be on my way." I wrote my name and phone number for Winnie and gave it to her. "If you need a ride, please give me a call. I live quite near you. And if there's anything else I can do."

"That's very nice of you. Thank you for driving me."

I patted her back, took my coat, and went to the door.

The younger Mrs. Platt followed me. "I appreciate your driving Winnie. She shouldn't take long walks at night."

I had no idea how to respond, so I didn't. I went out to my car and made my way back to Oakwood Avenue and completed my errand.

"That is one seriously weird family," I said to Jack when we were finally sitting in the family room sipping our coffee and eating the cake that I had picked up at Prince's.

"You're telling me this woman's son, the son of the murdered man, was working late on a Saturday night when he knew his father had just been killed and his mother was alone?"

"That's sort of what his wife said, but not exactly. When I asked if he was working, his wife said *no* and then changed her mind, as though I had given her the excuse she was looking for."

"Sounds like they should get the medal for dysfunctional family of the year."

"Frankly, my head is spinning from all of this. Forget about the mix-up this afternoon when I thought he was dead but he wasn't, don't families come together when a member dies? Even if this son, Roger, didn't get along with his father, he must have some feelings for his mother."

"I would think so," said my husband, who got along well with both his parents and would have broken speed limits to get to them if they needed him.

"And to walk on Oakwood Avenue at night. Jack, that's just looking for trouble. Wait a minute. She said something intriguing that I didn't follow up on. She said she didn't drive. Then she said she used to drive, but not since the accident."

"I'll ask at the police station tomorrow." He took an envelope that was ready to be tossed and wrote on the back of it. If there was a record of an accident locally, he would find it.

I started thinking that maybe I would drop in on the son and daughter-in-law the next afternoon and ask if there was anything I could do to help, and hope to pick up some sense of the relationships in the family. Then I had another idea. "Jack, when we finish our coffee, I think I'll take a drive back to the younger Platts' house. I'm a little concerned they may let Winnie walk home by herself."

"Come on."

"No, really. Neither one of those people went to get her or went to see her. Suppose she says she wants to walk and her son doesn't want to be bothered?" I took my last bite of cake and sipped my coffee. My usual nighttime sleepiness had fled. I felt very awake and very interested.

"Sometimes I wonder about you."

"Give me an hour," I said. "After that, I'll probably be glad to get home."

"Write down the address."

I checked it in the phone book and then wrote it down for him. He was clearing the cups and saucers as I put my coat on.

A large dark-colored car stood in the Platts' driveway. The living room lights were still on but I could see nothing through the curtains. I made a U-turn and parked a few houses back across the street, my car pointing in the direction from which I had come. If someone was going to drive Winnie Platt home, this was the way he would go. I didn't park across the street from their house because I didn't want to be noticed. Although it was dark and there were no streetlights, I knew that it was possible someone would look out a window or come home from a movie, see my car, and wonder what someone was doing there at that time of night. I would wonder the same thing on my block. In the suburbs people park in their garages or on driveways, and a car at the curb can be cause for concern. Our town has an ordinance against parking in the wee hours of the morning, which were still hours away, but I hoped no one would notice me.

I was there about half an hour when I saw the interior light go on in the dark car. They must have come out a side door, because I was watching the front door and it hadn't opened. I heard both doors slam shut and a moment later the car rolled down to the street and started toward Oakwood. I turned on my motor and went forward without my lights on till the Platt car turned at the corner. Then I turned my headlights on and took off after him.

He followed exactly the route Winnie and I had taken. I

could see them both in the front seat but they didn't appear to be talking. I worried about Winnie spending this terrible night alone in that big house. She had said she'd been married for forty-eight years. I wondered if her husband had ever left her alone during that time.

I kept well back on Oakwood Avenue and saw Roger's turn signal point left to the road up the hill. I was quite close to home now myself but my hour hadn't completely elapsed. I pulled over, getting the car off the road, and turned my lights and motor off. I had decided to follow Roger home, which meant I would have to make another U, but there was very little traffic.

Five minutes after he turned up the hill, the big car came down it. I started my motor as he looked left and right and then, to my surprise, turned into Oakwood Avenue away from his home. I pulled back on the road after he passed me, got my lights on, and kept following. He drove farther and farther from his home, eventually entering the town on the far side of Oakwood. He went into the center of town, made a turn, then drove into the entrance of an apartment complex. I followed him carefully, wondering who he intended to visit at this late hour, and saw him pull into an open parking slot, turn off his lights, and get out of his car.

He must be visiting someone, I thought. I turned my lights off but he seemed oblivious to me. He stopped under a bright lamp, put a hand in his pocket and pulled out a ring of keys. Then he walked to a door and let himself in.

Whoever Roger Platt was spending the night with, it wasn't his wife and family.

* * *

"Maybe that's where he works," Jack said.

"It's not an office building, it's an apartment complex. And it's expensive, Jack. If he just needed a room with a desk and a computer, why would he rent an apartment with a bedroom and kitchen?"

"Who knows? Maybe because he can afford it. Maybe it's their vacation getaway."

"April Fool, right?"

"Yeah. It sounds like these are very strange people. I feel sorry for that woman."

"Me too." I got the local phone book and looked up Roger Platt. There was one listing, the big house I had driven Winnie to. "I wonder if his wife knows about this apartment."

"Well, she sure as hell knows he's not coming home to her tonight."

"And he had no luggage with him. So he keeps clothes there."

"He may keep more than clothes there," Jack said.

"And no listed phone number. His wife said she reached him on his cell phone while he was driving to their house. Maybe that's the only phone he has. She may not know where he is."

"But she knows he's not with her."

"Very strange," I said. "But I'm too tired to think about it. And tomorrow is April second, so anything I hear I can trust to be accurate."

"Wow, do you have a lot to learn."

5

We picked up my cousin, Gene, on Sunday morning and took him to mass with us. Gene lives in a residence for retarded adults here in town, but for many years the home was in the town that the younger Platts lived in. We had decided to treat ourselves to an enormous buffet brunch at a hotel in that town. We had done it once or twice before, and thought Gene would appreciate it. For Jack and me it meant no more cooking or cleaning up for the rest of the day, a nice incentive after the great meal he had prepared the night before.

Gene was ready when we got to Greenwillow, dressed in slacks, a nice shirt, and a blazer. He carried a knit shirt with him so he could change and be comfortable when we got home after the brunch, and we stowed that in the trunk.

We got to church a little early. People were milling around outside, the first sunny Sunday we'd had in a long time. I said my hellos and listened to various conversations. They were all about the April Fools' Day murder, and one person seemed to know that there had been a false alarm earlier in the day when it was thought Willard

Platt was dead but it turned out he wasn't. I was glad my name wasn't mentioned.

We went inside and found a pew with room for four, Jack taking the outside aisle seat as he usually did, in case Eddie became obstreperous, although I must say he had been behaving quite well lately.

An hour later we piled into the car and drove to the hotel. It was a surprise for Gene, who was thrilled to pieces. After we were seated, I walked Gene around the buffet, showing him all the different foods, explaining that he could take whatever he wanted. It was his first buffet and he had a hard time believing that all of those wonderful-looking dishes were his for the taking. At one point he turned and spied the dessert table, his face lighting up. We walked over and he asked if he could have two desserts, and I said he could have two or maybe even three. He absolutely glowed.

I think I enjoyed watching Eddie and Gene even more than I enjoyed the food. Gene was especially taken with the scope and amount of food, sure that this could not last. He tried a few new things, and even admitted to liking the smoked salmon, but for the most part he stuck with tried and true favorites. And when we were ready for dessert, he almost went wild.

They had two huge containers of ice cream and all the fixings for sundaes. Eddie was satisfied with a scoop of vanilla and a taste of hot fudge, but Gene wanted everything they had, the whipped cream, the nuts, the sprinkles. He left most of it, although very reluctantly. But we promised we would come back for his birthday, and I think he started counting the days.

Full to bursting, we drove home. Eddie tumbled into

his bed, and even Gene nodded off on the sofa. Jack and I nearly giggled over it.

"Worth the price," he said. "I think this is a watershed day in Gene's life."

"I'm glad. Sometimes it's hard to think of what to do for him, but we've got the word now."

"Look, as long as everyone's conked out, I think I'll do some studying."

"Fine with me. I'm going to drive over to the younger Mrs. Platt's and see what I can find out."

"See you later."

I had thought Jack's days of studying were over when he passed the bar exam and became a lawyer, but he's an ambitious person, and having achieved one goal, he decided to pursue another. He has been a detective sergeant for years and is now studying for the lieutenant's exam, which tells me he's still happy to be part of the NYPD, something I wasn't sure of during the years he spent in law school. If he makes it—and I feel sure he will eventually—he'll be put on the civil service promotion list and get appointed when his number is reached. It will mean greater prestige, perhaps a new assignment, and a larger income. As a father, Jack is now looking ahead to sending our son to college, not the way he went, going nights for years while on the job, but registering and sticking around one place for four years.

At some point he will probably enroll in one of the prep courses given by retired chiefs and lieutenants that coach people for the exam. The classes are given days, nights, and weekends, so we'll go through that again, but he's waiting till he has done some work on the subject matter himself.

I thought about it as I drove to the Platts' house. Our lives are never static. I'm planning to change the course I've been teaching since I left the convent, as I don't want to grow stale, and with a small child, no day is exactly the same as the last one.

The large car that Roger Platt had driven last night was nowhere to be seen. I parked at the curb and walked to the front door, not altogether sure what I was going to say if Mrs. Platt happened to be home.

She was home, and she pulled the door open and looked at me with surprise. "Mrs. Brooks."

"Chris. Do you have a minute?"

"Well, I was going to go over to Winnie's to see how she's doing but I don't have to leave right away. Please come in."

"Thank you."

This time she took my coat and hung it in the front closet. She asked me if I'd like a cup of tea or coffee, but I was so stuffed from our brunch that I declined. We went into the living room and sat down.

"I was very concerned," I began, "when I saw your mother-in-law walking on that dark road last night."

"She doesn't drive. She stopped driving years ago. I don't think she even bothers to renew her license anymore."

"That's not the point. That's a fast road, there are no lights till you get right into the center of town, and frankly, I couldn't understand why no one picked her up to bring her over here." I knew I was talking about things that were none of my business, but I felt a woman's safety was involved, and I was hoping my hostess would let some interesting information drop.

"Roger was supposed to go there." She looked sad or distressed.

"But he didn't. It seems odd. His father was murdered yesterday. His mother is bereaved."

"I suppose to an outsider it might look a bit odd. My husband doesn't get along well with his parents, at least not with his father. The reasons go way back. I'm not sure I even understand them myself. Life isn't simple anymore. If it ever was."

"Is he on good terms with his mother?"

"Reasonably good terms. She's a nice woman and I feel very sorry for her. She lived with a difficult man and she gave birth to another one. Sometimes I think it's a miracle she's kept her sanity."

"She seemed very determined last night to see her son."

"She was. They had a good talk and then Roger drove her home. I'm going to see her this afternoon and bring something over that she can eat for dinner."

"By herself?" I asked.

"I think it's better that way."

"Mrs. Platt—"

"Doris. My name is Doris."

"Doris, I worry about a woman alone in that isolated location."

"Yes, I do too, but I don't know what to do about it at this point. I don't think she should come here."

"Doesn't she like it here?"

The question obviously disturbed her. "She wouldn't be happy here. That's all I can say."

I was starting to get a feeling about why that might be true. "Does your husband live here?" I asked.

"What?"

"I happen to know that he didn't come home after he drove his mother home last night. He went to an apartment in another town."

She looked at me as though I had just said something so incredible that she could not respond. "I don't know why you say that," she said finally. Now she looked scared. I had hit on something she didn't want to talk about.

"I was out last night and I saw his car come from Winnie's house. When it turned in the wrong direction on Oakwood Avenue, I followed it." It wasn't the exact truth, but it was close enough.

"My God," she whispered.

"Your husband doesn't live here, does he?"

She shook her head.

"Winnie doesn't know it, does she?"

"No." It was still a whisper. "Neither does anyone else."

"What do you mean?"

"No one knows. The neighbors don't know. My friends don't know. My mother doesn't know. My children don't know either."

"How old are they?"

"They're both out of college. They don't live at home."

"And when they visit?"

"Roger is here. He's here for his parents. If we're invited to a dinner party, he decides whether or not to go and we both go together. We've done this for a long time."

"Doris," I said, almost reeling from her admission, "do you know where Roger lives?"

She didn't answer for a moment. "I don't know where he's living right now. I have a phone number. I know where he works. This is the way he wants it."

I had a million questions to ask, but most of them were too personal and grew out of my curiosity, not my desire to find her father-in-law's killer. "I'm sorry," I said. "I know where he lives if you'd like the address."

She thought about it. "Yes, if you have it."

I wrote it down and handed it to her.

She looked at it and set it on the table nearby. "That's an expensive complex," she said finally.

"Doris, you said your father-in-law was a difficult man. Do you have any idea who might have wanted to kill him?"

She shook her head. "When I said *difficult*, I meant that he wasn't easy to live with. He was a demanding husband, or so Winnie seemed to feel. And Roger complained about him as a father from the day I met him. But there are many people who genuinely loved him. I know he had a good relationship with the high school drama society. He contributed to it so they could finance their plays. Some of the sets were expensive, and Willard wanted them to have the best."

"How did this relationship come about?" I asked.

"I think he did some acting as a young man. It was something that stayed with him. He and Winnie went into the city a lot for the theater. He wasn't interested in sports, either as a player or a spectator, but theater just captivated him."

"I see. He sounds like an interesting person."

"He was. Winnie will miss him."

I noticed she didn't mention Roger. "Last night, when I was driving her here, she said she hadn't driven since the accident. Can you tell me what happened?"

She looked uncomfortable, as though she didn't want to dredge up a past unhappiness. "She was driving and someone died."

I waited to see if she would tell me more, who the victim was, but she sat silently. "Who died, Doris?"

Her eyes filled. "My youngest child."

"Oh, how terrible." I felt a chill rush through my body. "I'm so sorry."

"It wasn't her fault. She picked him up from Boy Scouts because I asked her to. It was snowing and the roads were slick. She wasn't speeding or anything like that. They did an investigation afterward. But she lost control and skidded into a tree at the side of the road. Eric was killed instantly."

My own eyes were tearing at that point. She had described the worst of all possible disasters. "I'm so sorry," I said.

"That was the end of everything, the end of my marriage, almost the end of my life. Roger couldn't accept that it was an unavoidable accident. He blamed me for asking her to pick Eric up. He blamed Winnie for not driving well. He blamed his father for letting his mother drive, as though Willard could have prevented it." She looked thoughtful. "I suppose he could have. He was that kind of man."

"I'm sorry to have brought up these painful memories," I said. "Thank you for being so forthcoming. I think I ought to go home now. I guess I just thought there might be a motive for murder in something you could tell me."

"I don't think so. Roger stayed on somewhat good terms with his mother after that, although whatever warmth had been there was gone after the accident. But if you're thinking he might have killed his father because of it, I don't see that at all."

"Neither do I. I'm in the phone book, Doris. We're on Pine Brook Road. If you think of anything, please let me know."

"Why you? Why not the police?"

"Of course you should let the police know first. It's just that sometimes I look at things in a different way and I see things they don't quite get."

"I'll get your coat," she said.

6

When I walked into the family room, I could see Jack's papers where he had set them aside when Gene woke up and started to talk to him. I relieved Jack, who went upstairs to the study, and Gene and I played some simple games till I heard Eddie. When Eddie was up, I took him with me when I drove Gene back to Greenwillow. The first thing Gene did when we went inside was describe the buffet to the first person who would listen. We left him there and went back home, stopping at Melanie's house. There were no cars parked in the driveway that weren't hers so I assumed she had no company.

"Hello, hello!" she said when we rang her bell. "Come on in. I was just thinking about you guys."

"Where's Sari?" Eddie asked, pulling his jacket off. He felt as much at home here as in our own house.

"Right upstairs, sweetie. You know the way." She watched as he negotiated the stairs, then turned to me. "How was the brunch?"

"Fabulous. I had more fun watching Gene and Eddie than filling my face. What a great spread."

"It is great. Don't tell my kids you were there. We try to save that for special treats. Tea?"

"No, thanks. I'm still full."

"Then tea-less talk."

We had walked into the family room and plunked ourselves in our usual favorite chairs. "Tell me what you know about Willard Platt," I said.

"Oh, Chris, you're not."

"I am. This is a weird family, Mel. There are so many secrets and skeletons in their closets, I wonder if they check what they say before they say it."

"Really. Does that mean you have a suspect?"

"Not at the moment. Did you know Mrs. Platt was in a serious automobile accident some years ago?"

"I heard something. Wasn't a child hurt?"

"Killed. Her own grandson."

"Oh, my God. And she was driving?"

"Yes."

"How terrible. I wonder how she lives with herself. I could see that as a motive for murder, but—"

"Maybe a motive for murdering her," I said, "but not her husband."

"Anybody hate him?"

"The son didn't get along with him." I had decided not to publicize the details of the Platts' marriage. That was their business, and I didn't think it had anything to do with the murder of Roger's father. "But do you murder your father when you're almost fifty because you haven't gotten along with him for the last thirty or forty years?"

"Sounds like a stretch. If I were going to get rid of someone, I think I'd do it when the wounds were fresh and I was full of hate. After that you get to feeling—you know, why bother?"

"Exactly. So that's where I am. Have you heard anything through the Oakwood grapevine?"

"Nothing. I talked to some people, but all they said was what we already know, that he was murdered. It's such an isolated place, how would anybody get there without a car?"

I had asked myself the same question. "Suppose the killer walked up there?"

"People do it all the time," Mel said. "It's kind of a favorite hiking destination, the top of that hill."

"What's on the other side?" I asked.

"Got me. Let me think. It may still be Oakwood over there. I'll have to look at a map." She thought for a moment. "That is Oakwood, but it isn't very developed. One of these days some builder will come along and that'll be it."

I knew what she meant. All the open spaces were getting eaten up as the hunger for suburban houses increased.

We talked a little more about the murder, then about other things. I could smell her dinner in the oven and realized that although I had no intention of eating again today, most of the rest of the world was anticipating another meal. I collected Eddie and we said our goodbyes.

At home, Eddie ate a light supper and drank milk. Jack and I just passed.

"I made a phone call while you were out," Jack said that evening.

"In between entertaining Gene and studying."

"Yeah." He grinned. "Hey, Gene's no trouble. And I get a kick out of his observations. He sees life in a very interesting way. Anyhow, I called our favorite police department and asked about Mrs. Platt's accident."

"I've heard about it from the family. What did the police say?"

"It was an awful tragedy. Happened maybe five years ago. She had picked up her grandson to take him home and she hit an icy patch on Oakwood Avenue. I guess the car spun around or something and hit a tree. The boy was killed. She walked away with scratches but I'm sure her psyche suffered the kind of pain that will never go away."

"That's about what I heard. Her daughter-in-law, Doris, whose son it was, doesn't blame her. But Roger does."

"Look, I can't judge anyone in that situation. Something like that can make you crazy forever. And it's not a motive for anyone to kill her husband."

"The son blames him for letting Winnie drive."

"He may as well blame the car manufacturer. If you're going to kill, you kill the one who was behind the wheel."

"So this is all interesting but no motive. Do the cops have any leads?"

"Not that they told me. Frankly, I think they're looking at a blank wall. This is a guy who's got friends and enemies, people who can't stand him and people who think he's the cat's meow. What kind of a guy lies down on the cold grass waiting for a group of high school kids to find him and pull a fake knife out of his back?"

"I think I'll talk to Winnie Platt tomorrow. I've gotten her daughter-in-law's view of things. Let me see how that compares with her view."

"Way to go," Jack said. "I wonder if anyone's got his eye on the land up on that hill."

* * *

Monday is a day Eddie and I are home together, so I took him with me on the trip up the hill. I had no idea when the funeral for Willard Platt would be but it usually takes an extra day or so for the autopsy to be performed, and he had died on a Saturday afternoon. There was no chance it would be today.

As I drove up the hill past the nursery, I found myself hoping someone in the Platt family would be keeping Winnie company, but there were no cars in the drive when we got there. I parked outside the closed garage and Eddie and I walked up to the front door. I had some cheese, fruit, and crackers with me, and I had decided to ask Mrs. Platt if I could do some shopping for her.

"Mrs. Brooks," she said as she opened the door. "Come in. And you too, young man."

"This is Eddie. And I'm Chris."

"Yes. Chris."

I gave her the bag of food and she thanked me profusely. She was better dressed today, wearing a black skirt, a gray blouse, and a white cardigan sweater that looked expertly hand knit.

"I wanted to ask you some questions," I said when we were seated in a huge room with a cathedral ceiling and striking views.

"About what?"

"About your husband, his background, his relationship with the drama society."

"I don't understand. What is your interest in all this?"

"I happened to see your husband on the grass when he was waiting for the students in the treasure hunt. I called the police because I thought he was dead." I looked over to where Eddie was happily munching a cookie and playing with some things on the floor near the fireplace.

"I heard about that. I didn't know it was you."

"So when I heard later in the day what had happened, I felt a personal interest in the situation."

"Aren't you the one who brought Greenwillow to Oakwood?"

I hesitated a moment. That had been such a divisive battle the summer that I moved into Aunt Meg's house that I wondered if she would throw me out if she had been on the other side. There are still people in town who look the other way when they see me. "I was in favor of it, yes," I said honestly.

"It has worked out very nicely, don't you think?"

"Yes, it has."

"Did you know my husband?"

"No, I didn't." I decided not to mention Eddie's run-in with him some weeks earlier.

"I met him after the war, when he was studying in New York on the GI Bill. He went into the war a boy and came out of it a hardened man. He saw action in the Pacific."

"I'm sure that would harden anyone."

"Will was a tough man." She left it there, as though that were the final description of her husband.

"Tell me about the April Fools' Day treasure hunt," I said, just to get her talking.

"The drama club has been a favorite cause of his for years. He did a little acting in the late Forties and early Fifties, around the time I met him. I thought he would end up on Broadway or in Hollywood, but it didn't happen. He went into business instead, but he never lost his love of the theater. There were nights he went down to the high school when they were rehearsing and he read with one of the actors. He just loved it." She reached into a pocket in her sweater and took out a tissue, pressed it to her eyes, then put it back. "The treasure hunt was actually his idea, although the students didn't know it. I helped out on that myself. Wait. I'll show you." She got up and went to a drawer built into one wall of the room.

As she rummaged through it, I realized that there were many drawers, some of them the size of file drawers, and I wondered if this magnificent room might have been her husband's study. She came back with a folder and showed me a few pages.

"I wrote the clues for the hunt. Here's the one that Will took part in." She pointed to one of the short verses on the page.

Far away
And up the hill
Find a weapon
In back of Will.

"Do you understand it?" she asked.

"Yes. They were to find the stage dagger."

"That's right. Here's another one."

Quarter, dime, nickel, penny,
Jake has few, Jake has many.
If you are a sterling scholar,
He'll give you a silver dollar.

"Who's Jake?" I asked.

"That's what you have to figure out. Actually, this was

one of the easier clues. All the kids know Jake's place, even though it isn't called that. It's the variety store in town, where you can buy a newspaper or a lottery ticket or a birthday card."

I knew immediately which store she meant although I had never known the name of the man who owned it. "So they went there and he gave them a silver dollar?"

"After they said they were sterling scholars. That was the way it went. They had to interpret the verse, then they got the treasure."

"And you wrote all these little poems?"

"Will told me what he wanted and I sat down with a pencil and paper. It was fun."

"How did it work?" I asked. "Did every participant get all the poems?"

"No, they all got the first one. When they solved that, they picked up the next one where they got the first treasure."

"So someone had to go around to all these places and leave the poems and the treasures."

"That's right. Will and I did it on Friday. Everyone had already agreed to be part of it, so it was just a matter of driving around and leaving things in a bunch of places." As she described what they had done, her spirits seemed to rise. It was a nice memory, something she had done with her husband.

"How many students participated in the hunt?" I asked.

"I couldn't give you a number. I know there were three teams. One of them came in a van, one in a station wagon, and one piled into a car. But I don't know how many were on each team. And the clues were staggered. One team started with clue number one, one with clue number two, and so on, so they didn't get in each other's way and one team couldn't follow the other. I think there were eight clues, so the first team with eight treasures won."

"Did all three teams make it up here?"

"Yes. I know that because when the last one was gone, Will came inside to warm up and then he went out to the garage to get some work done. That's when it happened." She sniffed and bit her lips together. After a moment she said, "If you want the names of the drama club members, Mr. Jovine will have them. He's the drama coach at the high school. He's there every day."

I wrote it down, thinking I would have to take a drive over to the school. "Did he and your husband get along?"

"Mr. Jovine? Oh yes. Mr. Jovine loved Will. He knew if there was anything he needed, anything at all, Will would help."

"Was there a prize for the winning team?"

"I think there was, but I don't know what."

"Did you hear any cars come by after the last team left?"

"You ask the same questions the police did. No, I didn't. I didn't even hear the teams when they came. I was sitting back here and knitting. They were around the front of the house."

"Mrs. Platt, I heard that your husband made some demands on the town when they worked on the sewers."

"Demands? I don't recall he made any demands. He was concerned for our property. That same bunch had dug up someone's front lawn a year or two before and they never got it back the way it had been. And they weren't very nice about it. Willard didn't want that happening here. He just made sure they would replace anything they took apart."

She said it very matter-of-factly. Jack had said that the town paid for things they should never have paid for. I had no idea who his source was, but it always interests me to hear both sides of an argument. Mrs. Platt made it seem that they had asked only for what was due them. And if they had gotten more, could anyone in his right mind have killed Willard Platt for getting a few shrubs at the expense of the town?

"Mrs. Platt, I'm just trying to find someone who might have wanted your husband dead."

"Who could want such a thing?"

"Did he get along with your son?"

"They had a difficult relationship. They were two very strong-minded people. I don't think my son is happy his father is dead. Willard got along much better with our daughter."

"You have a daughter too?"

"Yes, but she lives outside of Chicago. She's on her way here now. She'll stay with me for a while."

"That's good. I'm sure she'll be a comfort to you."

"Do you want a copy of the clues for the treasure hunt?" she asked.

"Yes, I would."

"I'll make some." She took the sheets from the folder and went to a machine behind where I was sitting and I heard the sound of the mechanism. "I hope you can read them. They're from my originals and I wrote them in pencil."

"That's fine. Thank you very much." I folded them and

put them in my bag. I knew it was time to go but I hadn't learned very much about Willard Platt. "Do you have any idea who might have wanted your husband dead?"

She shook her head. "I loved him. I wanted him around forever."

"Someone he did business with? Someone he lent money to?"

"Will didn't lend anyone money."

"He walked with a cane," I said, remembering it from the supermarket and on the grass near his outstretched hand when I had thought he was dead.

"He had a weakness in one leg, going back to an accident a long time ago, before I met him. He could walk without it—he often did in the house—but he felt more secure if he had it. It was almost a prop for him. I think he liked to be identified as the man with the interesting cane. He had several. They're right over here."

I got up and walked over to a wooden rack near the back window. It held a collection of canes and walking sticks, most of them wood, some of them intricately carved, at least one made of what appeared to be ivory. I touched it, feeling its smoothness, seeing the grain. "These are beautiful," I said.

"He collected them. Most of them he never used, just enjoyed owning. Most of the time he alternated two or three favorites. The one he had on Saturday was a very plain one. He had to drop it on the grass and he didn't want a good one getting wet and trampled."

I lifted a briarwood stick with a large round knurled handle on top, then an old one with a tarnishing silver handle. These had surely come from abroad, from places I had never visited.

I wanted to ask about the old accident, but I felt I had spent enough time and worn her out enough. I asked if she wanted me to buy any groceries, and she thanked me and assured me that Doris had taken care of that. I told her to call if there was anything she needed or if she wanted to talk.

Then Eddie and I took off.

7

I have the world's greatest baby-sitter, my mother's old friend, Elsie Rivers. She substitutes for a grandmother and does a terrific job. When we got home, I called and asked if I could leave Eddie with her after lunch and she generously invited him to have lunch with her, something I knew he would appreciate. Since I am not very inventive where food is concerned, he gets much better fare when he sees Elsie. After I left him, I went home and called the high school. They have recently installed one of those terrible "press one, press two" systems that everyone deplores and everyone else seems to use. I went through the directions, eventually reaching Mr. Jovine's number. As luck would have it, he didn't answer in person but on his voice-mail machine. I left a message and decided that I would drive over to the high school whether I heard from him or not. Their day ended around three, and I would try to catch him before he left.

While I was eating my sandwich and drinking my tomato juice, the phone rang. It was Mr. Jovine.

"Thank you so much for returning my call," I said. "I wonder if I could talk to you this afternoon. It's about Willard Platt."

"Ah, yes. Well, I have a free period from one to one forty-five. Can you make it then?"

I looked at my watch. It was only a ten minute drive, probably less. "I can be there."

"I'll meet you in the hall outside the main office."

I gulped down my sandwich, drained my juice glass, and ran.

Oakwood High School sits on a beautiful piece of property in the heart of town. The building is set well back from the quiet road and is landscaped to provide a barrier between it and the occasional traffic. There are parking lots all around it, and I was surprised at how many cars were there. I guess if you're seventeen and don't have a car, you're just not with it.

It was a few minutes before one when I pushed one of the front doors open, looked around, and turned left into a long hall. The first door on the left was the administration office, and standing beside it was a thin man with a short dark beard.

"Mr. Jovine?"

"Yes." He smiled and offered his hand. "Mrs. Brooks?"

"Glad to meet you."

"Do you mind if we sit in the auditorium? My next class meets there."

"Sure. That's fine."

We walked back to where the hall started, turned left and went into a large, unlighted auditorium that looked very much like the one in my school twenty years ago. We walked down the center aisle, then up several stairs to the stage. I followed him into the wings, where he turned a light on. It was a cozy little area with an old oak table and a couple of chairs. We sat down.

"Are you a member of Will's family?" he asked.

"No. I'm a neighbor. I happened to be up on the hill the afternoon of the murder, when Mr. Platt was lying spread-eagled on the grass waiting for the drama students to find him."

He smiled. "Our treasure hunt. He was such a great sport. I don't know what we'll do without him."

"What exactly did he do for you?" I asked.

"The question is, what didn't he do? He helped build sets. He contributed generously when we needed to buy equipment or rent costumes. He came down and read with students who were trying to learn their parts. He kept us going is what he did." He seemed sincerely saddened by the loss.

"Do you have any idea who might have wanted him dead?"

"Not in a million years. I know he ruffled some feathers in town. He was a perfectionist in an era when perfection isn't even a goal anymore. He had fights with the mayor, he complained when a group of kids had an overnight near his house and left the place a mess. What's wrong with that? Who wants to wake up and find garbage near his property?"

"I understand. But being angry at things like that isn't really a motive for murder."

"Just what I'm saying."

"How long have you taught here?"

"Nine years."

"Then you didn't know the Platts' children."

"They're way before my time. I know the son doesn't

get along with the father, but that's not exactly news these days. Oh, and there was an accident. That happened several years ago."

"Tell me about it."

"It didn't involve Will. It was his wife. She was driving one of their grandchildren somewhere on a snowy day and somehow got involved in a one-car accident. The grandchild died."

"I see," I said. "How did Mr. Platt take it?"

"Very hard. He blamed himself. Said she drove a small car and he didn't think that was as safe as the car he drove, a bigger, heavier model. Also, he thought he should never have let his wife near the car on a day like that."

It's the kind of statement that annoys me, although I understood why Willard Platt had said it, if indeed he had. I can't imagine my husband forbidding me to drive my car if, in my judgment, I was able. But the Platts were older people and perhaps lived by a different set of rules. I wasn't about to argue. "There was another accident, wasn't there? Something that left Mr. Platt with a cane?"

"Oh that." He smiled. "That was before I knew him. I think he broke a leg. There are several stories about how it happened but the bottom line is the leg didn't heal perfectly. He could walk without the cane, but the truth is, he liked it, thought it made him look distinguished. He had a few of them, some of them hand-carved, real works of art."

"But you don't know how he broke the leg or when it happened."

"Not really. He never talked about it."

"How many students are in the drama club?" I asked, changing the subject.

"We have fifteen this year. Fourteen of them took part in the hunt. Robby McPhail didn't show up."

"Any reason?"

"I haven't seen him." He looked at his watch. "He'll be in my class in a few minutes. Maybe I'll ask him."

"Could I have a list of the members?"

"Sure." He got up and went to a phone. In a short conversation, he asked someone to make a copy and drop it off at the main office. "It'll be waiting for you," he said when he came back. "Can I ask you a question?"

"Of course."

"Why are you here? What's this all about?"

"I feel a personal interest, Mr. Jovine. I was very upset when I found Mr. Platt on Saturday afternoon. I thought he was dead and I called the police. When he was actually killed a couple of hours later, I couldn't believe it. I just want to find out what happened."

"So do we all, Mrs. Brooks. I've talked to the police and I think they've talked to most of the kids in the club. I don't think they've come up with anything."

"I haven't either," I admitted. "But I'm just starting."

"Let me know if you turn anything up."

I had used up most of the forty-five minutes and I didn't want to keep him. I thanked him for his time and asked if he minded if I talked to the members of the drama club. That was all right with him, so we shook hands and I found my way back through the auditorium to the main office. The woman behind the high counter had a couple of sheets of paper for me, which I tucked in my bag. Then I went home and started making calls.

Because the three teams hunted in a staggered order, team three should have arrived at the Platts' first and team one last. I started calling names on the team one list first, trying to find a parent at home. On the third try a woman answered.

"Mrs. Powell, this is Chris Brooks here in town. I'd like to ask you about your daughter's participation in the drama club treasure hunt last Saturday."

"What's your question?" she asked, sounding a little defensive.

"Who drove the car for Ronnie's team?"

"Ronnie did. She drove my car. It's a van. She's seventeen and it was daylight."

"I would just like to know who was in the car with her."

"I don't remember how they divided up. She'll be home from school by four. Would you like her to call you?"

I said I would and gave her the number. It was only a quarter after two, and whether Eddie was awake or asleep, I didn't have to rush back to get him. I went out to the car and drove to the apartment complex where Roger Platt lived. I parked near what appeared to be a central entrance and went in to look at the mailboxes. There were four buildings altogether but I didn't know which one I had seen Roger walk into, so I went through all the names. There was no Platt anywhere, no Roger as a first name. This man was certainly trying very hard to keep his whereabouts a secret. It occurred to me that he might not even receive mail at this address. People who didn't know he lived here would write to him at his wife's house. Others might be directed to a P.O. box, possibly with a fictitious name or even none at all.

I was about to leave when a man in work clothes came out of the lobby.

"Help you?" he said.

"I'm looking for Mr. Platt."

"Platt? No one here by that name."

"He lives over in that section." I pointed.

"Sorry. Better check the address."

"He's about six feet tall, nice looking, late forties."

"Sorry, miss. I can't help you." To emphasize that that was it, he walked away.

I went back to my car and drove to Elsie's.

I knew Jack would get the highlights of the autopsy report from someone at the Oakwood Police Department. He had a good relationship with them, and that was information they would be much more likely to give him than to give me. I assumed the autopsy would be today, so it was possible he might know something when he came home, but I didn't want to ask him at work. I took Eddie home and waited for a phone call from Ronnie Powell.

It came at four-fifteen. "Mrs. Brooks?"

"Yes. Is this Ronnie?"

"Yes. My mom said you called?"

"I wanted to ask you some questions about the treasure hunt on Saturday."

"That was so terrible, what happened. We didn't hear about it till later. That poor man."

"Ronnie, how many people did you drive to the Platts'?"

"Just four. There were five on team one and five on team two, but Robby McPhail didn't come in time so we went without him."

I looked at my list and checked the name. "Did he come later?"

"I don't think so. He wasn't in my car anyway. We waited five extra minutes and then Mr. Jovine said to get started."

"Have you seen him since Saturday?"

"Uh, no, I don't think so."

"Was he in school today?"

"I'm not sure. We don't have any classes together. I only know him from acting."

"Who were the other people in your car?"

"Karen, Steve, and Missie Carter."

Those were the other names on my list for team one. "Did they all go through the whole treasure hunt with you?"

"Uh-huh."

"When you left the Platts', were all four of you in the car?"

"Yes. Two in the back, two in the front."

"Where was Mr. Platt lying when you got to his house?"

"On the grass. He was, like, on his stomach and the knife was sticking out of his back."

"Did you see his cane?"

"Uh . . ."

I waited. "Ronnie?"

"I don't remember."

"Where did you park when you got to his house?"

"In the driveway. We all got out and ran over to him and Steve pulled the knife out. It wasn't a real knife, you know."

"It was a prop."

"Yeah."

The cane had been near his right hand and the driveway was to the right of the lawn where he was lying. If you ran from the driveway to his "body," you would almost trip over the cane. "You don't remember seeing it."

"No. It could have been there. I just don't remember it."

"And the other three team members definitely got in the car with you."

"Definitely."

"Thanks, Ronnie."

I put a check mark next to her name and wrote *absent* next to Rob McPhail's name. Eddie was playing contentedly so I called the number for Missie Carter.

She answered the phone a little breathlessly and said she remembered the visit to the Platts' house very well.

"Did you see the knife sticking out of his back?" I asked.

"Oh, yes. It looked so real it was kind of creepy."

"What about his cane?"

"What cane?"

"Mr. Platt always used a cane."

"But he was lying down."

"Did you see the cane anywhere near him?"

"I'm not sure."

"Who pulled the knife out of Mr. Platt's back?"

"Steve did." She was sure of that.

"Did you drive back in Ronnie's car?"

"Sure. We all did."

"Have you seen Robby McPhail since Saturday?"

"Uh, no. I don't know if he was in school today."

"Thank you, Missie."

I called Steve Wolfson and went through much the

same questions. He wasn't sure about the cane either but he had pulled the knife out of Mr. Platt and then they had taken off. "It's a speed thing," he volunteered. "You can't wait around because another team'll get to the finish first."

"So you were running all the way."

"Oh, yeah. We still had a couple of places to go and we'd had a problem before that, which cost us some time. We were really in a hurry."

"Where on the driveway did Ronnie park the car?"

"I don't know what you mean."

"Did she pull all the way up to the garage or park near the road?"

"I don't think she pulled all the way up. Like I said, we were racing against time."

That could explain why they hadn't seen the cane. The cane was out of reach of his right hand, closer to the house. If they had approached from where his legs were, grabbed the knife and dashed back to the car, they might not even have glanced over to where the cane lay.

I called Karen Harding, the last member of the team, and asked her the same questions and got the same answers. She just wasn't sure about the cane but she agreed they had turned into the driveway, stopped, emptied out of the car, run across the lawn, grabbed the knife, and made their getaway.

I knew I would have to call the other ten students who had taken part in the treasure hunt and ask them too, but first I called Mrs. Platt and asked whether she had the cane her husband had had with him on Saturday.

"No," she said cautiously. "Why do you ask?"

"I just wondered where it was."

"Does it matter?"

"Probably not," I said. "It just seemed a loose end."

But she was sure it had not been left behind when her husband's body was taken away. I then called Jack.

"Before you ask," he said, "the autopsy was this morning and I have a preliminary report, by which I mean some stuff was read to me over the phone."

"Good. Let's talk about it when you get home. I'm interested in something else at the moment. Do you know what things the police picked up at the crime scene? Like his wallet, his keys, his cane?"

"I didn't ask. You want me to give them a call?"

"If you have a minute. And one other thing. I don't know how far an autopsy goes, but I'd like to know what kind of damage one of his legs sustained to make him need a cane."

"I don't have that. I'll get back to them. I'm working my way through a very boring document. It'll be my pleasure."

My pleasure was to start dinner.

8

"So what would you like to know?" We had gotten the dishes done and Eddie to bed. The coffee was brewing in the kitchen, its scent traveling to where we sat. Jack took some folded paper out of his briefcase and opened it up. It had notations on it that I assumed had to do with the Platt homicide.

"Start with the property," I said. "What do they have?"

"No wallet, but that's probably because he was working in the garage. But his keys were in his pocket, a few coins, a couple of tissues, the watch he was wearing, and that's about it. They have his clothes and shoes, nothing out of the ordinary."

"What about his cane?"

"No cane listed."

"Mrs. Platt says she doesn't have it."

"Maybe it's still in the garage. He could have set it aside when he was working and the cops didn't see it. There wouldn't have been any reason to take it."

"I'll go up to the Platts' house tomorrow and see. Tell me about the autopsy."

He looked down the top sheet of handwritten notes.

"He was stabbed four times, one wound piercing his heart. He died quickly and bled profusely."

"Anything on the weapon?"

"Yeah, it's double-edged."

"How do you walk around with a double-edged knife?"

"I suppose it had a sheath of some sort. We used to see a lot of them back when I was a young cop. They fall into the dagger and dirk category of knives—needle point, slender, sharp edges."

"You're still young," I said.

"Yeah, but it ain't the same." He sounded almost wistful.

"A knife like that, it's really a weapon."

"You bet."

"So it wasn't that someone came along and had an argument with Willard Platt and pulled this thing out. Someone went over there to kill him."

"I'd say so. And maybe it wasn't the first time in his life someone tried."

"What do you mean?"

"Autopsies often turn up surprises. Your Mr. Platt took a bullet a long time ago."

"Someone shot him?"

"Sure looks like it."

That was a surprise. Then I had a thought. "Jack, he fought in World War Two. Could that have been when he was shot?"

"I'd have to ask the M.E. They said it was an old wound. I don't know if they can date it."

"Anything else?"

"I asked them about his legs. They didn't seem to have anything but they said they'd take some X rays and see if anything turned up. I'll hear tomorrow."

"Well, even without that, this has been pretty interesting. I wonder how many people are walking around with a healed gunshot wound."

At that moment the phone rang. I got up and answered it in the kitchen. It was Mrs. Platt.

"Chris," she said, "I went out to the garage after you called to look for Will's cane. There's no cane out there at all."

"I see. My husband talked to the police today and asked what possessions of your husband they had. There was no wallet."

"No, I have that. He left it in the house when he went out to work."

"And there's no cane."

She was silent for a moment. "I don't understand it. He had a cane with him when he was waiting for the drama students. I know because I saw it on the grass when I looked out the window. I'm sure he had the same one when he went out to the garage. Where could it be?"

"We'll have to find out."

"I'll look again, but I don't think it's there."

"Don't do it tonight, Mrs. Platt. It's late and dark and you must be very tired."

"Yes," she said as though she were far away.

"I'll talk to you tomorrow. Did your daughter arrive?"

"Oh yes. It's good to have her here."

"Good night then."

I grabbed the carafe of coffee and took it in to the family room, poured for both of us, and brought it back to the kitchen. "The cane's not in the garage," I told Jack.

"So it looks like our killer took it with him. Kinda crazy

thing to do. It isn't worth anything, and if he's stopped, it's evidence."

"Killers aren't the smartest people in the world."

"This one's pretty smart, or at least lucky. With three carloads of kids coming to that house, he managed to show up when they were gone."

"That was lucky," I said. Maybe he had been lurking around the area, although it wasn't an easy area to find cover in. But there were trees and shrubs he could have hidden behind.

But why? I asked myself. What could this retired grandfather have done to provoke someone to kill him? And where had his son been all that long afternoon? I would have to find out.

Tuesday is the day I teach at a local college. It's also one of Eddie's nursery school days. I asked Elsie to pick him up so I could get a few things done.

I had one of my good lunches at the college, prepared by the food service students, and picked up a fresh apple pie to take home. Then I stopped by the Platts' house.

A woman in her forties opened the door and introduced herself as Toni Cutler, the Platts' daughter.

"I'm Chris Brooks." I offered my hand. "How is your mother?"

"She's all right. I think we're all so dazed it hasn't sunk in yet. Are you the one who was looking for the cane?"

"Yes. The one your father was carrying last Saturday."

"Come on in." She turned toward the kitchen. "Mom? Chris Brooks is here."

Winnie Platt came out of the kitchen, drying her hands on a small towel. "Chris, I've been through the garage over and over. The cane isn't there. And it's not in any of the places Will ever kept them. What does that mean?"

"Someone walked away with it," I said. "Maybe the person who killed him."

"What would anyone want an old cane for?"

"I don't know." I turned to her daughter. "Can I drive you anywhere?"

"Oh, no, thanks. I have Dad's car and I've already been out to pick some things up. And Mom and I have arranged for the funeral."

"When will it be?"

"Thursday. The Medical Examiner's office will release the body either this afternoon or tomorrow morning. I've been trying to reach my brother but he isn't home, and Doris doesn't know where he is."

I had a pretty good idea but I didn't say anything. Apparently Roger hadn't let his mother know he had a cell phone. "I'm sure he'll come home for dinner," I said, biting my tongue. "Could we sit in the kitchen and talk for a moment?"

"Of course."

I followed Winnie Platt and her daughter into a palatial kitchen. My friend Melanie would probably claim it for her own if she saw it. It looked like a cook's dream. At one end was a round dark-stained oak table with matching chairs, and the three of us sat around it. "Mrs. Platt, I wanted to ask you about something my husband learned yesterday."

She looked at me expectantly.

"The Medical Examiner looked at your husband's body." I didn't want to be too graphic, but I was sure she understood what I was alluding to.

"I know that. I asked them not to, but in cases like this, it's the law."

"That's right. And he discovered an old gunshot wound." I stopped and let her absorb it.

"That's not possible," she said finally.

"My dad was never shot," Toni said. "We would remember."

"It was an old wound."

"Well, the war," Mrs. Platt said. "He was in the Pacific. I think I told you. He saw action. He never talked much about it but it's possible he was shot then. That was before I met him." Then she shook her head. "But I can tell you he never got a Purple Heart. I have all his medals."

"And you're sure nothing ever happened while you knew him?"

"Of course I'm sure. It's not the sort of thing you'd forget."

"In the last few weeks, did your husband seem upset about anything?"

"You ask the same questions the police asked. And I'll give you the same answer. He was himself. He spent a lot of time with the high school drama society—they're working on a play—and he did his usual things around the house. Sometimes he was grouchy, sometimes he was very happy. We were planning a trip for the summer. It was all very ordinary."

"Who brought in the mail?" I thought this was a good question because I'm the person who does it most days in our house and I see the envelopes before Jack comes home.

"Both of us. It just depended who went out for it first."

"Did you see anything unusual in the mail?"

"I don't think so. It's all bills and catalogs. We don't get a lot of letters. Mostly we use the telephone."

"OK," I said. "That's really all I wanted to ask you, that and the cane." I got up and we said our goodbyes.

At home there was a message from Jack and I called him back.

"Got a call about Platt's leg X rays. They show absolutely nothing, Chris."

"No breaks?"

"Nothing. The M.E. said he had two healthy legs. Now, that doesn't mean he didn't have arthritis or sciatica or something like that."

"But he wouldn't have had things like that as a young man, would he?"

"Probably not. Mrs. Platt tell you he always used a cane?"

"From the time she met him."

"Maybe it was an affectation. Maybe he thought it made him look distinguished."

"I guess that's possible," I said halfheartedly. "By the way, she doesn't know anything about an old gunshot wound. She thought it might have happened during the war but he never got a Purple Heart medal."

"Maybe they forgot to give it to him. I'll see you later."

I was making a shrimp dish for dinner and I decided to clean the shrimp before I picked up Eddie. I took them out of the refrigerator and got my special cleaning knife. As I poked it through the first shrimp I realized it was a kind of two-edged knife. That, of course, was one reason I kept it where Eddie couldn't possibly reach it. I looked at it, testing the edges carefully. It was surely one of the sharpest implements I owned, a very useful tool once or twice a month when I needed it, but potentially a deadly weapon. Anyone who carried around something this sharp and this dangerous could have nothing but malice in his heart.

Not long after I got back from Elsie's, Mrs. Platt's daughter, Toni, called.

"Mrs. Brooks, I'm sorry to bother you."

"It's Chris, and there's no bother."

"I can only talk a second. Can we meet tomorrow for a little while?"

"Sure. What time is good for you?"

"Ten in the morning?"

"That's fine. Where would—"

She interrupted me. "Outside Prince's. I'll see you then." She hung up.

I gathered she didn't want her mother to hear the conversation or to know she was meeting me. I wasn't sure what that meant, but I thought it was a good sign. Maybe she knew something that would help find her father's killer.

9

Elsie took Eddie in the morning, and I drove to Prince's, parking in their large lot. Toni Cutler was standing near the automatic doors and she waved when she saw me.

"Good morning," she said. "How about a second breakfast?"

"Sure."

"Let's go across the street."

We went to the Village Coffee Shop, a pretty place that served all day long. I had never had anything but coffee or a snack there but I thought that if I had something substantial, I might not have to make myself lunch, for me the most boring meal I eat every day. We sat at a table away from the windows—I had a sense that Toni didn't want to be seen, or perhaps didn't want to be seen with me—and she suggested pancakes and sausage.

"Sounds good to me," I said.

She repeated the order to the waitress and asked for lots of coffee. Then she turned to me. "Mom told me about what happened on Saturday before Dad was killed, how you came upon him by accident."

"I was very embarrassed," I admitted. "I got the police

up there for nothing. They were very nice about it but I'm not sure they appreciated an April Fool's Day prank."

"You did the right thing. I'm sure you know that. Mom knows about you because she's taught Sunday school at our church and she met the Grants. You helped out a friend of Amy's a couple of years ago."

"Oh yes. That was a very strange case, a tragedy that happened on Valentine's Day up near Buffalo."

"That's what Amy said. She couldn't say enough good things about you, Chris. She also told us you'd managed to solve some other murders that eluded the police."

"I have. With a lot of help from my husband, who's a detective sergeant with the NYPD, and also from my former General Superior at St. Stephen's Convent."

"Of course," she said, as though something had just cleared up for her. "You're the ex-nun."

"I didn't know *that* was well-known."

"But it is. I think everyone in town knew when the Greenwillow affair happened."

I smiled. "The Greenwillow affair" referred, I supposed, to the moving of Gene's residence into Oakwood and my part in getting it there. "And here I thought I was anonymous."

"Hardly," Toni said. "I want to tell you some things about my father, things I don't want to discuss with the police."

"Do they have a bearing on his murder?"

"I don't know. Maybe you can figure it out. Mom and I talked last night about what you said about the gunshot wound. I can tell you it didn't happen while Mom knew Dad, and that's a pretty long time, like almost half a century."

"Then it happened earlier. And your mother's probably right. He was in the war. He may have gotten shot."

"Dad has an old friend who lives in New York. They were in the war together."

"Interesting," I said.

"And they've been friends forever. Maybe he knows something that Mom doesn't know. Will you talk to him?"

"If you'd like me to."

"Good. I'll call him when I get home and set something up. I don't want my mother to know. She's very upset, as you can imagine, and she doesn't need anything else to worry about. My brother is enough of a worry at this moment."

"Is there a problem?" I asked innocently.

"I hope not. It's just that he's not available and he should be. I don't know why he's working so hard when his father has just died and his mother is grieving. It seems to me there are times that you set aside your work and put your family first."

I agreed with her but I didn't want to break a confidence. Maybe he just didn't want to be around his wife, I thought. "I understand he didn't get along with your father."

"That's true." The pancakes came, fragrant and warm, and she paused till the waitress left. "They look good, don't they?" She smiled and started buttering hers. "Roger and Dad never saw eye-to-eye on anything. If Roger wanted to read fiction, Dad thought it should be nonfiction. If Roger wanted to study German, Dad thought it should be French. I know these seem like petty disputes, but in my family they were magnified. Dad wanted Roger to become a doctor or lawyer; Roger majored in history and then kicked around for a couple of years doing nothing. My father thought that doing nothing was about the worst thing a young man could do. They stopped speaking to each other around then and they never really started after that."

"What did Roger do eventually?" I asked. I assumed he had a job. The house he owned cost a fair amount of money, not to mention the apartment that only his wife and I knew about.

"He went back to school and became a civil engineer. He said he wanted to build bridges and highways. But those first years were pretty boring and mundane and he left the company and got a degree in business."

"It sounds as though he's got himself a lot of education."

"He does, but he doesn't use most of it. Or maybe he does in a way. He's had a number of jobs with different companies, and I think he's done better every time he moved. He works in White Plains now, which isn't too long a drive, and he's been with them long enough that I think it's permanent."

"When did he meet Doris?"

"In his kicking around stage. She worked after they got married and he went back to school. She's a nice person and she's been good to my parents. Roger is lucky to have her."

The conversation was making me uncomfortable. I wasn't sure anyone in Roger's family was very lucky. "Is he coming to the funeral?" I asked.

"He'll be there." I had the feeling she had said something like that to him in the same tone of voice.

"Do you know if your father left a lot of money?" I asked.

"Probably. I suppose you want to know who he's left it to."

"I'm just looking for a motive."

"I'm sure my mother has control of most of it right now. Neither Roger nor I really need any money. My mother will be well taken care of, which is as it should be. Roger didn't kill my father, Chris. There was no reason to. Whether Dad left him anything or not, it wasn't enough to make a difference. And although Dad did his best to push Roger around when he was young, Roger learned how to live with that. He became his own man."

"I find it strange that Roger chose to live in a town so close to your parents."

"Roger grew up here. When he got the job in White Plains, this was a perfect place for him to live. Doris liked Oakwood from the first time she saw it."

I had no argument with that. I loved the town. It was small enough to get around, big enough to have the schools and libraries that were important to me. And most of all, it was on the Long Island Sound, where we could enjoy the beach and the water in summer. "And he was near his mother," I added.

"Yes."

"I know about the accident, Toni. Doris told me."

"It was so terrible." Her voice had dropped to nothing.

"What's the name of the man you want me to talk to?" I asked, anxious to change the subject.

"Harry Franks. He's coming to the funeral tomorrow morning but he doesn't want to go to the cemetery. He's getting on in years and isn't all that well. He said he'd stay in the house and wait for us to come back. That would be a good time, I think, to have a private talk with him."

I finished off my pancakes and poured a second cup of coffee. "I can pick him up at the church."

"Good. I'll call you."

I let her leave first. I went back across the street to Prince's and bought something. When I got back outside, Toni had driven away. I wanted to check some things out around where the Platts lived and I didn't want her involved. I drove to the nursery, situated just below the Platt house and on the other side of the road. I parked my car in their lot, got out and walked over to the road.

You could see the Platt property clearly from this vantage point. It wasn't that far away but it wasn't a place you would arrive at accidentally. I started up the road, keeping myself behind trees as much as possible. I figured that if I couldn't see the house, no one in the house could see me. I darted from tree to tree, coming ever closer to being even with the house. Unless someone were looking out a front window—or the garage, I thought—I was sure I was close to invisible.

Finally I stood where I was exactly opposite the front door of the big house. The garage doors were closed but they had likely been open last Saturday when Willard was killed. How would I approach so that he would not see me?

I walked farther up the hill, still using trees as my cover. Then I stepped out into the sunny road, crossed over, and started down the hill toward the driveway. I imagined the older man standing on the concrete floor of the garage, looking down at whatever he was working on. It was chancy, but by walking across the grass I could probably have made it almost to the garage before he looked over and saw me.

As I reached the driveway I saw the mailbox. Most of the houses in Oakwood are set fairly far apart and mail is delivered from a truck, not by a person walking. The Platts' box was a plain, old-fashioned metal box, similar to the one we have at our house. Something about it made me stop. The box was significant, I was sure of that, but how?

And then I remembered. When I had arrived at the house last Saturday, the red flag was up, signaling that someone had left mail to be picked up. Maybe the mailman had seen something.

I walked back down the hill to the nursery, got into my car, and drove to the post office.

"Bernie's the guy," the supervisor said after I had asked who delivered to the Platts up on the hill. "But he won't be back till he's finished his route." He looked at his watch. "Probably not till four."

"Can I call him here?" I asked.

"Yeah sure, but it's kinda busy here when the guys come back. You could come over and talk to him."

"I'll do that. Thank you."

I picked up Eddie and we spent the rest of the day together until four, when I drove us to the post office. The man named Bernie was already back from his route, and he came out to the area where the boxes lined the wall to talk to me while Eddie peered through the boxes at whatever was behind them.

"Yeah, I do that house. It's at the end of my route, that and the nursery. I heard what happened. Terrible thing."

"I was there earlier in the afternoon on Saturday," I said, "and I noticed that the flag was up. That means you hadn't gotten there yet. I wondered if you might have seen anything as you drove by, anything going on in the garage."

He thought about it. "They never put that flag up last Saturday."

"It was up in the early afternoon. I was up there and I saw it."

"That's really crazy. When I got there, I can tell you the flag was down. I got their mail together, opened the box, and there were all these letters they'd left for me to pick up. I thought it was strange. They always put the flag up when they leave something for me. But that time they didn't. Mrs. Platt, she doesn't drive, so if she's got mail to go, and she has a lot of it, she leaves it for me."

"How do you know she doesn't drive?" I asked.

"She told me. Long time ago. I been doing that route for years. She asked me was it OK if she put the mail out for me and I said sure, but don't expect it to go out today. She didn't care. She just wanted it picked up."

"So the flag wasn't up but she had left mail."

"Right. Like I said, it was a little bit strange."

"Was the garage door open when you drove by?"

"I really didn't notice. It could have been."

"Did you see anything unusual?"

"Nah. I just dropped off the mail and took off. That was my last stop. It was Saturday and I wanted to get home."

"Do you remember what time it was when you got there?"

"Musta been almost four."

"Did you see a car parked in the driveway or on the road near the house?"

"No. I would remember because I make a U-ie just above the house and come back down. There was nothing there."

"Thanks, Bernie."

I knew the red flag had been up, and if the Platts had left mail in the box, it should have been up. It was possible that one of the drama society kids had pushed it down just for fun, and I would have to ask them—all fourteen of them, I thought—if one of them had done it. If they hadn't, then it seemed to me that Mr. Platt had been murdered before the mailman drove by, and the killer had put the flag down so he wouldn't stop unless he had something to deliver. The killer could have supposed there was a chance that the Platts had no mail that day and that the mailman just drove up there to make his necessary U-turn and to check for outgoing mail. If Bernie had passed by a little before four, Willard Platt must already have been dead.

At home, I called team one first, as they were the last group up to the house, and asked about the red flag. Two of them remembered it had been up. Interestingly, they were the two riding on the right side of the car. The driver, Ronnie, and the person behind her had not noticed it at all, which wasn't surprising. The mailbox was on the far side of the driveway.

I decided not to call the other ten students. If the flag was up when the last team got there, it had to mean that the killer put it down.

* * *

As I worked on dinner, something came back to me about Saturday. When I had found what I thought to be Willard Platt's lifeless body on the lawn, I ran to the front door and rang and knocked, calling for anyone inside. No one had answered.

Winnie Platt had told me afterward that she was in the back room we had sat in and thus had not seen anything going on in the front. But not seeing and not hearing were two different things. I put down my vegetable scraper and called her number.

Toni answered. I explained what was troubling me.

"That's not surprising," she said. "Mom has a hearing problem in one ear. If she was sitting with that ear turned toward the front of the house, she wouldn't hear the bell. I've been standing a few feet from her and asked her something and she didn't hear a word."

"So she could have been there and not only didn't hear me but also didn't hear your father if he called for help."

"That's right. In fact, she talked about that last night, whether he had called her and she hadn't heard. She was troubled to think that might have happened."

So that answered that little puzzle. I told Toni I would be at the church to pick up Harry Franks tomorrow morning.

10

Thursday morning Eddie went off to nursery school. He had gotten an invitation to go to a friend's house for lunch and play afterward, so I was free to talk to Willard Platt's old friend without worrying.

I drove over to the church at ten-thirty, not sure how long the funeral would last, and parked across the street so as not to get involved in the many cars that would travel to the cemetery. When the doors opened and I heard the music, I got out and stood beside the car where I would be visible. A moment later the casket and the family came out. Toni saw me immediately. She said something to her mother, who stood beside her, and crossed the street.

"My brother didn't come," she said.

"Oh, no."

"Just didn't show up. It's worse than that. Doris said he never came home last night."

"I'm so sorry. You don't need any of these complications at a time like this."

"We'll deal with it somehow. Come with me. I'll introduce you to Harry. Then I have to run."

We crossed the street and Toni brought a small, thin man over to where I was standing. He had sparse gray hair and wore a tweed coat. I could see a black tie knotted on his white shirt. He looked sad and tired and older than Willard Platt.

"Chris, this is Dad's old friend, Harry Franks. Harry, this is Chris, the woman I told you about. She'll take you to the house."

"Fine, fine," he said. "Pleased to meet you."

I put my hand through his arm and led him across the street. He seemed frail, almost bewildered. When he was in the front seat, he sighed and stretched out his legs.

"I'm glad this is a car. All the ladies in this town seem to be driving trucks these days. They're a bitch to get into."

I smiled. "I'm happy with a car, Mr. Franks. Can you get the seat belt OK?"

"Oh yeah." He pulled at it and clicked it in place. "Call me Harry. It's what I respond to."

"OK, Harry. We'll go back to the house."

We left before the line of cars had finished forming. I noticed the mayor and his wife get into one, and I remembered what Jack had said about Willard Platt demanding a bond and landscaping for work the town did near the Platt house. Were he and the mayor on good terms in spite of that? I wondered.

"Nice town," the man next to me said. "Last time I was here, Will and Winnie took me out to a great restaurant somewheres along here. And I slept in their guest room. Felt like a king. It's bigger than my whole apartment."

"It's a beautiful house," I agreed. "How long have they lived here?"

"They built it after they were married. Gotta be a long time ago. You hear what happened?" He turned to me.

"No. What?"

"Roger didn't show. Can you believe that? Didn't come to his own father's funeral."

"Maybe you can tell me a little about their relationship."

"Doesn't matter what their relationship was. Your father dies, you come to the funeral. I didn't always get along with my old man, but when he died, I was there. And it wasn't for the money because there wasn't any. He died and I picked up his debts."

I turned up the road to the Platts'. "I agree with you. It's the right thing to do."

"I don't understand it. I just don't understand it."

I turned into the driveway, thinking I would be better off with the car on the road when the time came to leave, but I didn't want this old man to have to walk. As I came to a stop at the closed garage, he unbuckled his belt and opened the door before I could get to him.

"I got the key," he said, taking it out of his pocket.

We went inside and hung up our coats.

"Winnie said to put the heat up," he said, walking into the living room. "I got it. Seventy OK for you? Winnie says it goes higher than where you set it."

"Seventy's fine."

The living room was huge but the furniture was arranged so that we could sit in a small area just made for a few people.

"You want to talk to me about Will."

"You knew him longer than anyone else."

"We were poker partners in the war. Made a lot of money between us. It wouldn't sound like much to you, being as you're so young, but to us it was more than we'd ever seen in one place at one time."

"Did you meet in the army?"

"Navy," he corrected me. "We were sailors. You should've seen us in our uniforms. We were really something."

I found myself liking this man very much. "Would you like something to eat or drink?" I asked, not sure I could find anything.

"A cup of coffee would really hit the spot."

"Let me see what I can do." I got up and went to the kitchen, Harry trailing me. There were stacks of dishes and silver on the round table we had sat at the other day, in anticipation of the guests who would return after the visit to the cemetery. A coffee maker stood on the counter, and in the refrigerator I found several pounds of coffee. I measured that and the water and turned the machine on. In a minute we could smell the results.

I took two cups and saucers from the table and poured for us. "Anything to eat?" I asked.

"Coffee's enough. Thanks. You're a good girl to do this for me."

Back in the living room, I opened my notebook. "Do you know if Willard was shot during the war?"

"Never. Neither was I. The good Lord was watching over both of us, but don't ask me why. We didn't deserve it any more than anybody else. We saw a lot of fine people die, young fellas that would have been fine old men if they'd been luckier."

"I'm glad you and Will made it," I said. "What did you do with your poker winnings, or did you spend it while you were in the Navy?"

"I saved every dollar of it, and so did Will. When we got back, I bought my mother a house. She wanted a house all her life and couldn't ever afford it. Will put his in the bank. When he and Winnie got married, he used it to build this."

"A good investment," I said. "I'm sure your mother must have been very happy with the house you bought her."

"She was, very, very happy, God bless her."

"Did you marry, Harry?"

"Oh yes, married a good woman, but she's long gone. I've got a daughter who's good to me. And two grandsons."

"That's wonderful."

"Sure is." He drank his coffee almost as if it were cold water, in big gulps. I was glad I had made more than a couple of cups.

"You said Will wasn't wounded during the war."

"That's right."

"Was he ever shot after the war that you know of?"

He pushed the cup and saucer away from him, as though now that he had finished, he wanted nothing more to do with it. "You want me to tell you the truth, right?"

"Please do."

"Something happened. I can't tell you what, I can't even tell you when. It was after the war and before he met Winnie. Winnie was a beautiful girl, by the way. Just a beauty."

"What was it that happened?" I prompted.

"Oh, the gunshot. He told me afterward, there had been a fight of some kind. We didn't see each other every day or every week, you understand. We saw each other once in a while, so if something happened, I might not hear about it for a long time. He said someone pulled a gun and he got shot."

"Did Will get along with Doris and the children?"

"Oh, yeah. He loved them all. He'd talk about how great those kids are." He looked over at me. "You heard what happened? The accident?"

"I heard, yes."

"Terrible thing. Terrible, terrible thing. He never got over it."

"Did you know Roger well?"

"Can't say I did. I knew them as children but I didn't have long meaningful talks with them when they grew up." He smiled. "Kids aren't too interested in sitting with Dad's old friend and talking. They'd rather be out throwing a ball."

The doorbell rang and I jumped.

"That'll be the food. They're deliverin' for the company, when they get back from the cemetery. It's all paid . We just have to put it in the kitchen."

e went to the door together and let the caterer in with ber of platters and boxes. I signed that it had been d and Harry reached into his pocket and pulled bills as a tip.

e on our way back to the living room when "You ever see Will's cane collection?"

howed me some of them the other day."

me."

the beautiful back room where I had and Harry went over to the stand with d one out, a walking stick with a silver unscrew the top. "See this?" he said. e off, and when he pulled it out of aw that a knife was attached to it.

"Did you ask him more about it?"

"I asked him but he didn't tell. Said there was nothing to it. He was fine. 'Forget it, Harry. There's much more important things to worry about in life than a little scratch.' "

I could hear his voice change as he imitated his friend. "And that was it?" I tried to hide my disappointment.

"I'll tell you one thing. It was after that that he started carrying a cane."

"He was shot in his leg?" I asked with surprise. That was not what the autopsy had said.

"No, no. He was shot here, in the midsection somewhere." He rubbed his hand over his belt. "I don't know exactly where. I never saw the wound. But that's when he started walking with a cane."

"So maybe wherever he was shot, it made it hard for him to walk."

"I don't know. It's kind of a mystery to me, always has been. He walked like his leg bothered him, but he was shot somewhere in the middle. There were a lot of mysteries about Will. Tell you the truth, I always thought it could be his ex-wife that shot him."

That perked me up. "Will was married before he married Winnie?"

"Oh yeah. When he was a young guy, just outta the Navy. He met this girl, real whirlwind courtship. They got married, settled down, and then it was over."

"How long were they married?"

"Not long. Maybe a year. They fought like cats and dogs. At least, that's what he told me."

"Did you meet her, Harry?"

"Oh yeah. I was his best man. They were married downtown by a justice or something. I went down with them, and her sister came too. At least, I think it was her sister. Then the two of them, they flew outta that place and dashed off on a honeymoon. That was probably the best two weeks of their life together. I don't think things went too good after that."

"Do you remember the date they got married?"

"Hadda be 1946. Spring, I think."

"And you think she may have shot him?"

"I could believe it," he said, leaning over to look at his empty coffee cup.

"Let me get you some more coffee," I said, picking up his cup and taking it to the kitchen.

I got us both coffee, glad to see there was still some left in the carafe in case Harry wanted more. I had the feeling it cranked him up, and things were getting interesting.

"Ah, that's a good girl," he said when I got back. "It keeps me going, that stuff. I don't listen when the scientists talk about whether it's good for you or not. I'm old enough now, it won't hurt me if I drink what I like."

"Did they have children?" I asked, sitting down.

He looked at me somewhat wide-eyed. "Now that's a good question. They weren't together long enough for more than one, but to tell the truth, I don't know the answer to that. He never said they did. 'Course, he never said they didn't."

"Do you remember her name, Harry?"

"Amelia. Amelia McGonagle, or something like that. She'd be Amelia Platt though, after they were married. And she was young and cute. She probably married again after they split up. Maybe more than once. Who knows?"

"So when Will started going out with Winnie, he was already using a cane."

"I'm pretty sure of that."

"Did Winnie know he was married before?" I asked.

"Hah." He put his cup down and looked at me. "The truth is, I couldn't tell you, but I don't think so. Will said not to talk about it so I never did, but that doesn't mean she didn't know."

"So you don't know."

"Not for sure, I don't."

"And it's possible, even if Winnie knows, that Roger and Toni don't."

"You're askin' a lot of questions that give me the creeps, you know that?"

"I'm trying to find out who killed Will."

"I understand. And you probably know more right
than the police do. But I don't know all the answe
I knew Will one hell of a long time."

"I'd like to ask you about Roger."

"Ah, Roger." He shook his head.
his own father's funeral. What is th

"Did something happen bet

"It was a clash of perso
to explain it. Sometim
gulped his coffee
as he had befo
thing. Wil
He's a

"But y
had."

"Everything
agreed on anyth
could do no wrong
just think Roger shou

"You bet. Wanna see another one?" He took a carved cane at random, unscrewed the hooked part, and drew out yet another blade, thin and threatening.

"Are they all like that?" I took one and looked at it carefully, trying to find the break in the wood. It was there. I could feel it with my finger.

"Every damn one. He never bought a cane that didn't have a sword or bayonet in it. You wanna know what I think?"

I leaned forward to hear.

"I think he carried these things for protection."

"Against what?"

"Who knows? Maybe against whoever it was shot him."

"Like his first wife?"

"Maybe. Maybe it was someone else. I don't think there was a goddamn thing wrong with his leg. I think he made it all up. He wanted an excuse to carry a cane, that's all it was."

And in that moment I realized how Willard Platt had been murdered and why his cane was missing.

11

We talked a little longer and finished the coffee. I washed out the carafe so the Platts could use it and I checked to see whether any of the food that had been delivered needed to be refrigerated. Harry grew tired and leaned back and closed his eyes. I could have left, but I decided to wait with him till the family returned.

He fell asleep where he was sitting, but he slept fitfully, muttering unintelligible words from time to time and thrashing around with his hands. Finally I heard the sound of a car door slam and I got my coat and went to the door.

Mrs. Platt looked ready to collapse, but Toni was in good shape and helped her mother inside. I expressed my condolences again and went outside. Doris and her children were just getting out of their car, and several more cars were making their way up the hill.

I took off. It had been a fruitful meeting with Harry. Whether Wilbur Platt's first wife had shot him or not, the discovery of the secret of the canes had been worth the effort. The more I thought about it, the more I was sure Harry's interpretation was correct. Willard Platt carried a cane for protection. His legs were fine, maybe even perfect. But he was an actor and he had spent the better part of his life acting the part of a man with a weak or an injured leg. I wondered whether his wife and children knew that it was all an act. Winnie had said that he didn't really need a cane, that he just felt more secure using one. He didn't use one in the house. But I was ready to bet that he kept one next to his bed in case of attack.

But attack from whom? Surely his ex-wife was not going to come out to Oakwood fifty years after marrying him to settle some old score. And any child who might have been born during or just after the marriage had not shot him.

But what was now quite clear to me was that whoever had killed Willard Platt had done it with his cane. Perhaps Willard, sensing an attack, had unscrewed the top of his cane and tried to intimidate or harm his killer, who got the upper hand and took the cane with its lethal double-edged sword and stabbed him with it. His protection had become his undoing.

Or did the killer know from the outset that the cane contained a knife? Did Winnie know? Did Roger know?

I pulled into my driveway and went inside. I opened a can of my favorite soup and heated it up. Where was Roger? I wondered. I thought of driving over to his apartment, but I still didn't know exactly where he lived and I didn't want to knock on doors and ask questions that would blow his cover. Still, it made me uneasy that he had disappeared. So what if he didn't get along with his father? His father was dead. He could be a good sport and go to the funeral. But he hadn't.

I sat down with my good-smelling hot soup and a glass of tomato juice and opened my notebook. I would have to look up Amelia Platt in our phone books, although I had little hope of finding her. I turned a page and began to wonder whether the police knew about the canes. There had been no mention in the autopsy report that the double-edged blade that killed Willard came from a cane. If there had, Jack would have been sure to tell me.

I started thinking again about how the killer had gotten to the house and away from it. He could have screwed the top of the cane back and walked away as though it were his. Or he could have chucked it in the back of his car and driven off. Or he could have continued up the road and over the top of the hill. A weekend hiker would have no difficulty doing that.

Winnie and her children had to know about the canes. Harry knew, which meant Will had told him. Surely Will had told his wife. Maybe he had not told his children when they were young to keep them from harm, but at some point they must have found out. I would ask Toni.

I was a little sorry I hadn't gone to the funeral and seen who was there. I had been a bit surprised when the mayor and his wife came out of the church, but Willard Platt had been a fixture in Oakwood for so long, it made sense that the mayor would pay his respects, even if they'd had their differences.

I looked at the names in my notebook. Mr. Jovine would have no motive whatever. Indeed, unless Willard had put something in his will endowing the drama society, their bounty may well have dried up. It was impossible to believe that one of the fourteen students had killed Willard. Only one of the four in team one would have had the opportunity, and it would have been very difficult to accomplish.

There was Bernie, the mailman. Kix, I said to myself, you are really stretching.

I kept coming back to Roger. But it didn't make sense. Roger had a screwed-up life, but killing his father would not make it better.

I got up and gathered up the telephone books of the five boroughs. Jack keeps them current, so they're always a good source. I looked up Platt in Manhattan and almost gave up. There were a number of A. Platts, but no Amelia. Nor was there an Amelia McGonagle. I decided if I had nothing to do for a couple of hours, I would make some phone calls, but it didn't seem like a productive thing to do right now.

Instead, I called the house where Eddie was spending the day and asked how things were going.

"Just fine," Bonnie Wilson said. "I think they're still good for a while."

"I might go out," I said.

"Don't worry. I won't panic if you're not there."

That sounded good. I called the mayor next. I didn't really know him, but I knew he knew who I was. He was home and he said I could come over if I wanted to talk.

Mayor Herbert Strong and his wife lived in a medium-sized house on the other side of town. He was in at least his second term of office and I had never heard anything very good or very bad about him. I'm not very political, and the things I care most about, after the schools and the library, are keeping snow off the streets in winter and having a responsive police force. We have those things, so I'm a pretty contented resident.

The development in which the Strongs lived dated

back several decades. The houses were all built as small one-story affairs, each with a single car garage at the side. Over the years, the owners have transformed the little houses so that the area is hardly recognizable as a development. Many of the houses now have second stories. Most have two-car garages. Decks and additions have been built out back. It always pleases me to see that what some people sneer at as cookie-cutter housing can become so different, a reflection of the individuality of their respective owners. I think it says something wonderful about Americans.

The Strong house was one of those with a second story, the ground floor bedrooms having been converted into a large family room with a brick terrace outside. Mayor Strong and I sat there, facing the glass doors, and Mrs. Strong retreated to another room.

"I saw you at the funeral this morning," I said.

"Were you there? I didn't see you."

"I was waiting outside the church. I was picking up Mr. Platt's oldest friend."

"Yes, I saw him with the family. This is a very sad affair and a great loss for our town."

I wondered. "Tell me what you know about Willard Platt, Mr. Mayor."

"Well, he's lived in Oakwood much longer than I have. Must be close to fifty years. We've only been here about thirty. Years ago he worked in the city, but he's been retired or semiretired for a long time. He's been a big help to the high school, as you may have heard."

"I have heard," I said. "I also heard he's been a difficult person."

"Well . . ." The mayor smiled. "Let's just say he's looked out for his interests vigorously, as we all should."

"Did it cost the town much to protect those interests?"

"If you expect me to speak ill of the dead, Mrs. Brooks, you'll go away disappointed. Willard Platt was a good man and let's leave it at that."

"I'm trying to figure out who might have wanted to kill him."

"Let the police do their job. They're good at what they do and very dedicated."

"Whose feathers may Mr. Platt have ruffled?" I asked.

"There were some lawsuits I know of."

"Who did he sue?"

"The nursery for one."

"The nursery," I repeated.

"Will owned the land on both sides of the road."

"I didn't know that."

"He bought it years ago when you could have an acre for a song. He talked about developing the land one day, but he never did. He just thought it was nice not to have any nearby neighbors. The Vitales owned the land across the road at the bottom of the hill and opened for business a number of years after the Platts built their house. The nursery got pretty successful—they draw customers from all over—and they wanted to double in size. That meant buying land from the Platts, and Willard said no. The nursery offered a pretty good price for that land, but there was no deal.

"Then the Vitales started using some of the land just above their building so they could stock more trees. Apparently, they went over the property line and Willard was furious. He called them up and said to get off his land, and they said it was theirs—well, you can imagine it was a mess."

"Whose land was it?"

"Turns out it was Willard's. He had the old survey and it was pretty clear the nursery had gone over the line, not just a foot or so, but a lot. They tried to make a deal to rent the land or just to use it till he wanted it back, but he refused. He said if he let them do that, they might claim it as their own someday. There are cases like that, you know. He said he just wanted what was his, and when they wouldn't remove their plants, he hired a lawyer."

"Did it go to court?"

"The Vitales backed off, but Will said they had to pay for his lawyer."

"Ouch," I said.

"Exactly. They refused and he sued them. In the end, they paid up."

"What about the bond he made the town put up?"

"That was after the nursery fight. I think he was afraid of getting burned. We put up the bond, there was no problem. And we had to do a little landscaping on his property when we were finished with our work."

He was certainly making it all sound inconsequential. "What were your relations with Willard Platt?" I asked.

"We were on the best of terms. Next question?"

"Do you know anything about why he walked with a cane?"

"I assume he had a problem. He was never without it. Why would you ask that?"

"Because the autopsy showed nothing wrong with either leg. And no one who's known him for a long time can remember anything happening that might cause him to need a cane."

"We weren't close, Mrs. Brooks. It's not the kind of thing you ask a man about. You just accept that he has a problem and leave it at that."

"His wife was in a terrible car accident some years ago. What can you tell me about that?"

"Just that it was terrible. It was a snowy day in a cold, bitter winter. I remember that winter well. My mother, God rest her soul, slipped on some ice outside her house and fell and broke her hip. She was never the same after that and she died a sad woman, unable to do all the things she had been doing with so much pleasure for so long."

"I'm sorry to hear it. Were there any charges filed against Mrs. Platt?"

"Not that I'm aware of. She's had to live with great unhappiness since that day. I don't think putting her through a trial would have done any good."

I had begun to sense a defensive demeanor in the mayor. His usual ready smile was gone and he was speaking in a manner that indicated he wished I would get up and go. I decided to oblige him. "Thank you very much for your time." I stood and shook his hand, a limp handshake if ever I'd had one. He raised himself from his chair and walked to the coat closet with me. His wife appeared from wherever she had been hiding and I thanked them both for letting me come.

I made up my mind that I didn't like him very much.

Late in the afternoon, after I picked up Eddie, I called the Platt house and talked to Toni. "Is there any word on your brother?"

"Nothing. I told Doris I thought we should report him as a missing person, but she doesn't agree."

I could see why. "He's probably just overwhelmed by what happened, Toni. Maybe he's sitting in some little place thinking about his relationship with his father."

"That doesn't sound like the Roger I know. Tell me, did you learn anything from Harry?"

"A few things. I'm glad we got together. He's a very nice man and he cared deeply for your father—and for all of you. He told me something quite fascinating about the canes."

"That they open?"

"Then you know."

"Oh, yes. They were Dad's pride and joy. Some of them are very valuable, hand-carved, silver tops."

"And they all have sharp-edged instruments inside."

"Yes. Dad kept us away from them till we were old enough to be trusted. Then he showed us. We were forbidden to play with them, as you can imagine."

"Toni, the cane your father had out in the garage the day he was killed is missing. I think the killer used it and then took it away with him."

"I— Wait a minute. What you're saying is that the killer knew the cane had a weapon inside. You think Roger did this."

"Not necessarily," I said, although Roger was certainly a likely suspect. "It's possible that your dad saw someone coming or got into an argument with whoever was there, pulled the knife out of the cane to protect himself, and the killer wrestled it from him."

"I see." I let her consider this. "So it could have been someone who didn't know about the cane."

"That's right."

"Which means we're back where we started."

"I'm afraid so. Did your father let many people in on the secret of the canes?"

"No. I'm not surprised Harry knows, but Dad kept it in the family. I think he felt it was like money. It wasn't anybody's business but his."

"How is your mother doing?"

"We're all pretty low. She's very upset about Roger. Doris hasn't the faintest idea where he is. I have the strangest feeling something is going on, but I don't know what."

"How long are you staying?"

"Till the weekend. I'm going to have to arrange to have my mother picked up so she can do her shopping and get around. She keeps telling me she can walk—and I know she's done it—but that's not what I want for her. I'm afraid we'll have to talk about selling the house, but that's just too traumatic right now."

I told her we would be in touch before she left and I got off the phone. Eddie was exhausted from his long day and I thought it would be a good idea for him to eat and go to bed before Jack came home. As it happened, he agreed with me.

12

I finished my rather long narration after dinner.

"You've learned a hell of a lot in one day," Jack said. "Talking to the old friend was a real brainstorm."

"I can't take credit for that," I admitted. "Toni suggested it."

"You've got a lot of good stuff. The canes, the nursery, the first wife."

"I wish I felt it was leading me toward a killer. It's nice to learn interesting things, but I'm no closer to figuring this out than I was yesterday."

"Hey, you've got a bunch of new suspects—the owner of the nursery, this mayor you think was telling you what you want to hear. How about the bereaved wife?"

"Winnie Platt? That's ridiculous."

"It's not so ridiculous. She admits she was in the house that afternoon but claims she didn't hear when you rang the bell and called."

"Toni said she's deaf in one ear."

"Fine." He dismissed the excuse. "She was there, she knew that whatever cane her husband had out in the garage had a weapon in it. She could go out, unscrew the top, and stab him with it. Or she could take one off the rack you described, go out with just the knife portion, take it back inside, wash it, put it back on the rack—hey, why not?"

"Then where's the one her husband had with him?"

"Maybe that's back on the rack too. Maybe she wanted someone to discover that the cane in the garage was missing so they would think that an outsider came along, used it to kill her husband, and took it away."

"That's a very frightening scenario, Jack."

"Fits the facts," he said philosophically.

It did fit the facts and I didn't like it at all. Whether Winnie was hard of hearing or not, she was in the house at the time of the murder. I didn't have a motive for why she did it, but she certainly had the means and the opportunity. It answered the question of how the killer got there without being seen, the choice of weapon, the time it happened.

"Who found the body?" Jack asked.

"She did."

"No one else could have, right?"

"Right." They lived alone. There were no neighbors. There were acres of empty land and the nursery down the hill. "She would be crazy to do it."

"Why?"

I hate it when he asks why at times like this. "Because she would be an obvious suspect."

"It wasn't obvious to you. It wasn't obvious to the police. You all assumed she was a bereaved wife whose husband had been murdered by an outsider."

Jack has never been easy to argue with. First, he had all those years of police experience. Now, as a new lawyer, he has honed his argumentative skills—sometimes I think he's honed them using me—and left me feeling he's clever but I'm right, even if I can't prove it. "She didn't do it because she would be worse off without him than with him."

"Says who? She's got a house that she can sell for a lot of money. He's probably got a nice nest egg stashed away that she can live on. Think about it."

I didn't want to. "She loved him, Jack," I said.

Jack leaned over and gave me a kiss. "That's just what she would want you to think."

"It has to be someone else," I grumbled. I looked at my watch. "Jack, I'm going to take a drive over to the apartment complex where Roger lives. He's still missing, as far as I know, and I'd just like to see if his car is there."

"OK. Watch yourself."

I gave him a kiss, got my coat and went out to the car. I started with a short detour to check out the Platts' house on the hill. Many lights were on and there were several cars in the driveway and on the road in front of the house. That meant there were visitors, and I was glad to see that. Just to make sure I wasn't on a wild goose chase, I checked the cars for one that looked like Roger's. There were a couple that might have been his but neither had his license plate. I made my U and went down the hill.

Five minutes later I pulled into the parking lot where Roger had parked the other night when I followed him home. There were a lot of cars and I drove slowly, looking left and right for his. And then I saw it. I breathed a sigh of relief. Roger wasn't missing. He was just staying home. I followed the drive around the buildings until I found the exit. Then I went home.

* * *

Jack was dismayed when I asked him about trying to trace Amelia Platt, Willard's first wife. If they had married in the Forties, it was the era of paper records, none of which had ever been put on a computer.

"You could try Arnold," he said. "I know he's done some digging into the dim distant past. Maybe he'll give it a try."

I hadn't thought of that but he was right. Arnold is my lawyer friend whom I met back when I was single and newly out of the convent. Besides the fact that I love him dearly, he's got the sharpest mind I've ever had the pleasure to encounter.

He answered the phone himself and we chatted about families and weather and a case that was currently in court and being discussed in all the media.

Finally I said I had something to ask him.

"So it wasn't just a friendly call. You're breaking my heart."

I laughed. "Put it back together, Arnold. Something interesting has happened here in town."

"Don't tell me."

"Yes. A local man was murdered twice, and yours truly didn't know the first time was an April Fools' Day joke."

"You're confusing me. He was murdered twice?"

"Sort of. The first time was a joke, the second was the real thing. I talked to an old friend of his this morning—they go back to World War Two together—and the friend tells me the victim had a wife briefly after the war."

"And you want me to dig her up and find out if she killed her ex-husband half a century later."

"Well."

"What do you know about her?"

"She was Amelia McGonagle until she married Willard Platt. Her sister was supposed to be the second witness—the friend I talked to this morning was the first—and they were married at City Hall. Maybe I could locate the sister," I said halfheartedly.

"Any children of the marriage?"

"We don't know."

"You have a date for the wedding?"

"Spring 1946. Probably," I added.

To his credit, he didn't laugh out loud. But he groaned. "I don't know. When your own friends come at you with an impossible job, you gotta wonder. I tell you what. I've got a law student doing some work for me. I'll tell her if she's got any extra time, maybe she'd like to dig around in old records, if they haven't disintegrated by now. Anything else you know?"

"The marriage didn't last long, maybe a year, and sometime around that period, Willard was shot." I told him the rest of the story.

"Well, my young intern will have a good time with this. Who knows? Maybe she'll get hooked and you'll get your answers before I get mine."

"I like your spirit, Arnold."

"Spirit's about all I've got left."

Jack was studying for his lieutenant's exam, so I left him and called Doris Platt. It rang several times and the answering machine had just responded when she picked up. She was slightly breathless.

"I just came back from Winnie's," she said. "I hated to leave her, but Toni's still there."

"I wanted you to know that I drove over to your husband's apartment and saw his car there."

"I can't talk about this right now," she said, and I realized her children had returned for the funeral.

"I understand. I just wanted you to know."

"Thank you, Chris. The truth is, I feel better knowing it. I had no idea where—" She let it hang.

"Right. That's all. Good night."

" 'Bye," she said.

I then hauled out the New York City telephone books and started telephoning A. Platts in Manhattan. Without exception, they were all men. By the time I got to Brooklyn, one or two were women, and the same was true in the other boroughs. But there was no Amelia. It then occurred to me that she might have kept Willard or W for the phone book listing, so I looked for those entries. There was actually one Willard Platt on Staten Island but the man who answered was young—I could hear children in the background—and he had never heard of Amelia. He volunteered that his parents were named Harry and Sheila.

Disappointed, I continued, knowing that if I had the time, I could try all the Platts in New York, but being me, I worried about the phone bill. Each would be a toll call, as we lived in Westchester County, almost an hour from the city.

When I had covered the W. Platts in the whole city, I gave up. It was late by then, too late to decently call anyone, and I knew it was a lost cause. We live in a mobile society. A woman splitting up with her husband in the late Forties might decide to try her luck in California or Boston. The chances of her still being in the same city after so many years was very small. Willard had moved,

Jack had moved when we were married. I took the phone books and put them away.

"Did you really think you'd find her?" Jack asked.

"I had a faint hope. It's kind of silly. If she'd wanted to kill him, she would have done it long ago. But I'd really like to know who shot him and why."

"If it was his wife, it could have been a domestic fight that was over after she fired. Even if he went to a hospital to have it treated, he might not have identified her as the shooter."

It was all true. "And it was so long ago."

"I'd be looking for someone with a newer grudge. This was the kind of guy who could generate a long list of possible suspects."

"Like Mr. Vitale at the nursery. I'll have to talk to him. Maybe I'll go over there tomorrow. We haven't set up a date for them to plant our Japanese maple."

But the idea of the nursery owner killing Wilbur Platt because he wouldn't sell them land or let them use his land didn't really grab me. For something like that, you stop speaking to a person or you say nasty things about him. You don't kill. Somebody had to have a better motive than that.

13

What troubled me was Jack's almost convincing argument that Winnie Platt was a suspect. She was in her seventies, she had been married for more than half her life. She had a husband who, although he might be difficult to live with at times, was apparently faithful to her and a reasonably good companion. They had built a beautiful house together and had enjoyed living in it. She had convinced me, in our conversations, that she was sorry he was dead.

And looking at her situation from a less emotional and more practical viewpoint, it seemed incredible to think that a woman who no longer drove and who lived in an inaccessible place would deprive herself of the one person who could chauffeur her around.

When the breakfast things were taken care of and Jack had left, I got Eddie and myself dressed for the day.

"Would you like to see the tree I bought for us?" I asked him.

"What tree?"

"Daddy and I thought it would be nice to plant a Japanese maple tree in front of the house. It's just a little tree now and we can watch it grow."

"I like trees," Eddie said.

"I'm glad to hear that. I like them too. Let's take a drive over to see our new tree."

As I turned into the nursery drive I thought I saw a car backing out of the Platts' drive and then turn up the hill. I couldn't think why anyone would be going up there, but I couldn't stay and watch. I parked and took Eddie by the hand and walked down to where our little tree, a red and yellow SOLD sign still tied to it, sat balled and bagged.

"That's our tree," I said. "Isn't it pretty?"

"It doesn't have any leaves."

"The leaves will come out in the spring, honey. In a few weeks all the trees will have leaves. This one will have red leaves."

"I like red leaves."

I took my agreeable son's hand and walked back up the hill to the main building. I knew who the owner was, and we walked through the building till I found him. He was on the phone and I waited, looking at boxes of grass seed till he got off. As I saw him talking, I realized I could have called the police from here on April Fools' Day, but my mind hadn't been functioning well.

"Mr. Vitale, I'm Chris Brooks," I said as he hung up. "I'm up here to arrange for my tree to be planted."

"They can take care of that where you check out."

"OK. I'll talk to them on my way out. But as long as I'm here, I wonder if I could ask you a few questions about your neighbor up the hill."

"Like what?" he asked defensively.

"What kind of person he was. What you thought of him."

"He was a mean old man who'd squeeze you dry if he

could. I had dealings with him over the years, none of them good. Nothing was ever good enough for him. Nothing was ever right."

"What kind of dealings?" I asked, surprised that there might be more than the one thing I had heard about from the mayor.

"Years ago he asked me to plow out his driveway in the winter. It was a good deal for me. I had the truck. I did my own drive and it wasn't much to go up the hill and do his. You think it ever went right? He'd show me how I didn't get the last two inches on the right and left. He'd deduct a couple of bucks from the price we agreed on because I left a strip of snow an inch wide. The man was a weasel." You could hear the anger in his voice. "A petty weasel," he repeated.

"I heard you had a problem over land," I said.

"I guess everyone's heard about that. I offered to buy an acre just up the hill. Platt owned the land on both sides of the road up the hill from us and we really needed that acre. He drove a hard bargain, but I agreed to it. I arranged to borrow the money. Everything was go. At the last minute he changed his mind, pulled out completely. He didn't want to sell and that was that. I had incurred all kinds of expenses but what did he care?" He shook his head. "I don't know what I'm getting so worked up about. I can't be the only guy he stiffed. Someone else got to him last weekend."

"I know."

"Can I ask what your interest is in all this?"

"The Platts have asked me to look into the murder. You're his nearest neighbor. I thought you might be able to help."

"Wish I could. I'd like to pat the guy who did it on the back." His phone rang again. "Talk to the girl on the way out. I think the ground's still too hard to do any planting."

He picked up the phone as I took Eddie's hand.

As I drove out of the nursery, I looked up the hill and saw the same car, still driving up the road. I thought it was odd, but I turned toward Oakwood Avenue and took Eddie to do some food shopping.

When we came home, he helped me put things away and I made some egg salad for our lunch. When it was in the refrigerator, I pulled out my class's papers, which had to be corrected before next Tuesday. I had hardly looked at the first one when the phone rang.

"This is Toni," the caller said in a tense voice. "Something has happened. Can you come over before I call the police?"

"My three-year-old is here. Can I bring him?"

"Sure. Mom'll watch him while I show you."

"I'll be right there."

We were there in five minutes. Toni had the garage open and the door to the inside opened as soon as I parked.

"Come this way," she called.

We went through the garage and then inside, and Mrs. Platt took over Eddie in a grandmotherly way while Toni and I went to the door to the basement. She flicked a light on and we went down the stairs, very nice stairs considering they led to a basement. I saw why when we got there.

Almost the entire area, an area the size of the entire house, was finished. There were several rooms, including a bathroom, a place to play pool and pinball, to watch television, dance, read, or do other entertaining things. And there was a kind of pantry with shelves against the wall holding neatly arranged canned goods that could carry a family through an Arctic blizzard. Nearby were a washer and drier, some cabinets, and kitchen appliances that might not be used very often, like a coffee urn that could turn out coffee for a large crowd.

Adjoining this room was a workshop with a lighted table, tools, some lumber, plastic containers of nails and screws, and garden supplies that included an electric clipper.

"Over here," Toni said. She stepped over some things on the floor and said, "Here."

I followed her finger and gasped. On the floor, not well hidden, was a wooden cane. "Is that the one . . . ?"

"Mom says it is."

"How did you find it?"

"Mom came downstairs a little while ago to get a screwdriver. There's a door handle upstairs that needs some attention. While she was looking, she saw it."

"Did anyone touch it?"

"I didn't. Mom says she didn't." When I didn't say anything, she said, "I know it looks like someone with a key brought it down here, but that's not necessarily true. Look up there."

I followed her finger to a window near the top of the wall.

"It's open a little. Someone could have walked around the house, seen the window ajar, and put the cane through the opening. Anyone could have done that," she said pointedly.

That was true, but I was suddenly gripped with the fear that Jack's scenario was correct. Mrs. Platt had murdered her husband, tossed the cane down here under the window, and then conveniently "found" it today. "Yes, of course," I said. I knelt near the cane, looking for a crack near the top to show that it could open. The crack was there. There was a weapon inside and I was sure Willard Platt's blood would be on it.

"Do we have to call the police?" Toni asked.

I kept my shock to myself. "Yes, you do," I said. "It's been missing and now it's been found. It may have been a murder weapon. You have to call them."

"Let's go back up." She turned lights off as we retreated to the stairs.

On the main floor, I could hear Mrs. Platt and Eddie having a conversation. We stayed in the kitchen.

"Who has a key to this house?" I asked.

"Chris, no one in the family did this."

"The police will ask you."

"I do, Roger does, Mom and Dad. I don't think there's anyone else."

"Does anyone come and clean the house?"

"Yes, but Mom is always here."

"You'd better call the police," I said.

She remained at the table, looking unhappy. "I know this looks bad for Roger, but he didn't do it."

"Has he turned up?"

"Not that I know of. Mom and I are very upset about it. I called his work and was told he had asked for a few days off because his father had died. Of course they gave it to him."

I felt that my presence wasn't needed there anymore. I had told Toni to call the police. If she didn't, Jack or I would. I was sure she understood that without my saying it explicitly. It was almost lunchtime anyway and Eddie would be getting hungry. "I think it's time for me to go," I said. And then I remembered what I had seen earlier. "Tell me, when I was at the nursery this morning, I saw a car pull out of your driveway and go up the hill. Do you know who that was? There's nothing up there to drive to."

"That was Mom and me. Mom's going to start driving again. She hasn't been at the wheel since that terrible accident and she just wanted to reacquaint herself with the car. I sat next to her and she drove up and down the hill, made some turns, that kind of thing. She did very well. I think that's going to solve a very big problem for her."

"Does she still have a valid license?"

"Yes. It turns out she kept renewing it. I think she'll do fine. She won't have to take those awful nighttime walks anymore, even though she said she enjoyed the exercise."

The news didn't make me particularly happy. "That sounds good," I said halfheartedly. "She'll be able to keep her independence."

"And that's so important when you get older," Toni said, as though she really knew what it felt like.

"I'd better get Eddie home for lunch," I said. "I appreciate your calling, Toni. This is really a very important discovery. Are you leaving tomorrow?"

"Sunday. Thanks for everything, Chris." She offered her hand and we shook. "I hope you come up with something. I keep telling myself Mom is safe here, because she wants to stay and it's her home. If the police have learned anything, they haven't confided in us."

Nor in us, I thought. "They probably don't have anything. There are no neighbors here to see a car or a stranger walking."

"You know, I've been thinking about the cane. I don't think a lot of people knew about the canes having knives inside, but if Dad sensed a problem, he could've pulled out the knife and then had it used against him."

That had been one of my theories. "We won't know till we find out who the killer is."

We found Eddie and Mrs. Platt, both seemingly enjoying themselves. I told Mrs. Platt to call if she had any problems I could help with, and Eddie and I took off.

I hated to think that Jack was right, that Winnie Platt was a viable suspect, but this new development certainly pointed in that direction. The cane I had seen in the basement was either the same one I had seen on the lawn or one that looked very much like it. And Winnie knew the secret of the canes. I had only her word that she hadn't heard me ring and knock at the front door when I saw her husband lying on the grass. By her own admission, she was in the house at the time of the murder. She could so easily have walked out to the garage, taken the cane from wherever Willard had left it, taken out the knife and plunged it into him. She could then have taken it down to the basement, left it where we found it, and opened the window slightly to allow for the possibility that someone else had flung it through the opening.

Until the moment I knew she still had a driver's license and was planning to resume driving, I had a good case that she had not done the homicide. Now it didn't look that way anymore. Now it looked as though she might well have played the greatest April Fools' Day joke of them all.

14

When Jack called in the afternoon, I told him what had happened.

"I think Mrs. Platt ought to get herself a lawyer at this point," he said. "I'd say she's our best suspect."

"There's something else though. I think the story the mayor told was a sanitized version of what happened between Willard and the nursery. The mayor talked about disagreements. Mr. Vitale said he and Willard actually had a contract that Willard pulled out of. And it cost the nursery because they'd hired a lawyer and arranged for a loan."

"You're telling me he's a better suspect than he was yesterday."

"Right. Except for one thing. He didn't have to make Willard look as bad as he did. If he was trying to protect himself, he could have just glossed over everything. He even said if they found a killer, he'd like to shake his hand, or something like that. I don't think I'd say that if I was the killer."

"You never know. But OK, you've got two people with let's say equal opportunity. They're both practically on the spot. One knows about the cane, the other doesn't, but

I'd bet Vitale could overpower Willard Platt without much difficulty. And he could walk up there and not be noticed, dump the cane through the window, and get back in about ten minutes from start to finish."

"I'll keep them both on my list. I wonder if Arnold's intern will dig anything up."

"Don't count on it. He'll probably get bogged down in dust and bureaucracy."

"She."

"Ah. She. Then maybe you'll get something."

I smiled at that and went back to my class papers.

Later in the afternoon Toni called. "The police were here," she said. "I thought they'd just take the cane and leave, but they stayed a long time. They took pictures and they tried to take fingerprints off the window frame."

"They have to do that," I said. "I'm sure your mother's and father's prints are all over them."

"They would be, yes. I just wonder who else's are there."

"Any word on your brother?"

"No." She sounded very down.

"He'll turn up when he's ready." I said it as though I believed it, but down deep I wondered if he might be planning to leave the area or if he had already done so. Doris must have had a terrible time explaining things to her children, but by now was probably an expert at manufacturing excuses for why Daddy wasn't where he should be.

"I hope so." Toni sounded very worried. "I'm starting to be concerned for his well-being."

"Whatever you do, don't report him missing to the police till you check with Doris. She's his wife."

"Yes. Thanks, Chris."

I felt bad when I got off the phone. Toni sounded so low. She had so many things to contend with, and even if she didn't perceive that her mother might be a suspect, she had lost her father and, in a way, her brother. And if Roger didn't turn up, the well-being of Mrs. Platt might fall heavily on Toni's shoulders. Although Doris had seemed to be a concerned daughter-in-law, I wondered if that would be enough for Toni.

I didn't get any more news till Jack came home, and as usual, we waited until Eddie was off to bed before talking.

"I talked to the Oakwood cops before I left. No question the cane is the murder weapon," he said. "Not that that's a surprise, but it just confirms what we've been thinking."

"Is there blood on it?"

"Some. And the shape of the blade matches the wounds. They're checking out prints on the cane. Maybe that'll tell us something."

"I want to find Roger," I said. "If he's still in that apartment, he should turn himself in to the police."

"Why? He's not even a suspect."

"He is in my book."

"I guess you could knock on doors."

"How did I know you would say that?"

I didn't want to knock on doors, but I couldn't think of any other way to find him. I didn't want to do it at night, which gave me a convenient excuse to wait for tomorrow, which was Saturday. I pulled my papers over, as Jack was deep in the newspaper, and the phone rang.

"I don't know how you do it," Arnold Gold said. "You must just get the better cases."

"What's up?"

"My intern hit pay dirt. I can't say she did as well looking for what I needed, but something about the Forties just captured her imagination."

"You mean she found something?" I said.

"I've got the date of the marriage ceremony and the names of the witnesses."

"Arnold, that's wonderful."

"Tell it to my client who's still waiting for this intern to turn up something that'll save his cookies. Got a pencil?"

"You bet."

"One witness was Harry Franks. He the guy you already met?"

"Yes."

"The other was Maureen Benzinger. I'd say that last name is good news. If the bride's maiden name was McGonagle and Maureen was her sister, Maureen must've already been married, so there's a chance you can find her with that name. Her address at that time was in the Pelham section of the Bronx." He dictated it. "They did a lot of building out that way after the war. Maybe she got into a new apartment and decided to spend the rest of her life there. Lots of folks did."

"Arnold, this is just great. I can't tell you how much I appreciate it. Tell your intern—"

"To get on the stick," he interrupted me, "and do some of the work I pay her to do."

"I'll take you both to lunch next time I'm in New York."

"What? Tuna on white bread and a glass of milk? I'll take you. Don't forget. It's a date."

"Thanks, Arnold."

I went for the Bronx phone book the minute we were off the phone. I found a couple of Benzingers, neither at the address Arnold had given me, and I wasn't sure if either of them was in the right geographical place. That's the kind of thing Jack knows best so I bothered him with it.

"This one looks right," he said, pointing to J. J. Benzinger on a street I had never heard of.

"Well, here goes." I went to the kitchen and dialed the number. When a man answered, I said, "I'm trying to reach Maureen Benzinger."

"She's resting right now. Can I help you?"

The voice sounded more like that of a son than a husband. If this was the woman I was looking for, she'd have to be about seventy and could be more. "I'm trying to locate her sister Amelia."

"Just a minute."

I heard a woman's voice from a distance, then his. After a brief conversation, he came back. "My mother'll pick up. She can tell you whatever she knows."

I waited and finally heard a woman's voice. "Mrs. Benzinger, my name is Chris Bennett," I said, using my maiden name. I understand you're Amelia's sister." I didn't want to say Platt.

"That's right. Do you know her?"

"No, I don't. I need some information about her ex-husband."

"Barney?"

Oh gosh, I thought. Amelia's had more than one. "No, Willard."

"Willard? Willard Platt?"

"That's right."

"That was an awfully long time ago. I haven't thought about Willard for years. They were married just after the war."

"That's the one. Could you tell me where your sister is living right now?"

"She's got an apartment a few blocks from me, but I have to tell you, she isn't doing very well."

"I'm sorry to hear it."

"But you know, I bet she'd like the company. Here's her number." She dictated it from memory and I wrote it down quickly. "But don't call tonight. She'll be sleeping. She isn't well."

"What's a good time to call?"

"Oh, tomorrow morning is fine. She's up and about by nine."

"Thank you so much, Mrs. Benzinger."

"Well, I just can't imagine why anyone would be interested in Willard Platt."

I laughed when I got off the phone. "I found her, Jack," I called as I went into the family room. "She's alive and not very well and lives a few blocks from her sister."

"It's your magic touch. That's an easy place to get to from here. You don't have to go all the way into the city. Parking'll be a problem, but what else is new?"

"I'll call her first thing in the morning."

I was so energized by the discovery that I was up early, even though it was Saturday. We all ate together and then I called the number Mrs. Benzinger had given me.

I realized the moment the phone was picked up that I

had not asked for Amelia's current last name. "Is this Amelia McGonagle?" I asked, for want of a better name.

"Well, no one's called me that in fifty years but I guess that's who I am," a rather thin voice said. "Who are you?"

"My name's Chris Bennett. I talked to your sister last night and she gave me your number. I wonder if we could talk—"

"About what?" she asked tartly before I could finish my sentence.

"About Willard Platt."

"Willard? Why in God's name would anyone in his right mind want to talk about Willard Platt?"

"Something's happened and I need some information. I wonder if—"

She stopped me again. "You'll have to come here. I'm not feeling too good and it's hard to hold the phone."

"When is good for you?"

"One o'clock?"

"One is fine. Where do you live?"

She described it the way people who don't drive give directions. I jotted down what she said, knowing that Jack would have a map that could help me.

"And your last name?" I asked finally.

"Chester," she said. "L. B. Chester next to the bell."

"I'll see you at one."

15

I decided finding Roger would have to wait. I dashed out to do some shopping and put together lunch. I ate mine early, then drove to New York. Jack had located the street, just a few turns off Pelham Parkway, a wide road packed with cars. When I finally found Amelia's street, it was one-way the wrong direction and I wasted several minutes trying to get myself to her building by trying one narrow parked-up street after another and nearly losing the right one in the process. Then I made circles looking for a place to park. Finally, someone pulled out of a space just as I approached and I was able to squeeze in before the aggressive car behind me took it away.

I was two blocks from the address I was looking for, and I found L. B. Chester when I got there. Up on the fourth floor, Mrs. Chester opened her door and looked me over. "What did you say your name was?"

"Chris. Chris Bennett."

"Come in. You can leave your coat wherever you want. I can't hang things up anymore. Coats are too heavy." She had a walker that she leaned on wearily as we went into her living room. She shuffled in slippers although she was fully dressed and rather garishly made up with powder and rouge and a bright lipstick that looked very out of place. "Sit down." She motioned toward a sofa and set herself down in a chair with arms.

She was very thin, her arms bony, her fingers almost skeletal. Her eyes seemed to be set too deeply in her wan face and she had outlined them with dark pencil. I didn't think it added to her looks.

"So what's the story on Willard?" she asked when she had settled herself.

"Willard Platt was murdered a week ago today," I said, stopping for effect.

"Hah!" she said, a grin spreading over her face. "I knew someone would get him eventually. Just took some time."

"What would they be getting him for?" I asked.

"For being a mean bastard. That's enough, isn't it?"

I wasn't sure that it was. "Was he mean to you?" I asked.

"Mean as they come. I hated him."

"But you married him."

"I made a mistake. I met a gorgeous guy in uniform and I fell for him. He was big and strong and handsome and he swept me off my feet. That's why I married him."

"And then?"

"And then . . ." she said. She leaned back in her chair and closed her eyes. "It all changed. He changed. He didn't like the way I kept the apartment. He didn't like the way I cooked. He didn't like me to be late from work because then dinner was late and he was hungry and it was all my fault."

"It sounds like you weren't suited to each other."

"No kidding?" She paused for breath. "Who'd he marry?"

"A very nice woman. I've only just met her. They live in my town."

"He never made it to Hollywood, did he?"

"I don't think so. Did he talk about it when you knew him?"

"That's all he talked about. I didn't think he was such a great actor, but he did. He was good-looking enough, I guess. Nowadays that's all it takes, but back then you had to have talent. He didn't have any."

I thought it was her anger speaking, not her judgment. If Willard had convinced everyone he knew for fifty years that he had a bad leg, he was a pretty good actor in my book. "I think he went into some kind of business," I said. "But he worked with high school students in the drama club."

"Good for him," she said sarcastically.

"Did you and Willard have any children?" I asked.

"Did I have a kid with Willard? Who gave you that idea?"

"I'm just asking. If there were a child, he might have some claim on Willard's estate." I didn't know if that was true, although I thought it likely, but it seemed to me if she was reluctant to admit the existence of such a child, an inheritance might change her mind.

"He leave a lot of money?"

"More than I have."

"More than I have too, I bet."

"Did you have a child together?"

She closed her eyes for a moment, then pulled a tissue

out of a pocket and patted her nose. "I got a kid, but it's not his. He was my first husband, not my last."

OK, I thought, then no claim on the estate. "When was the last time you saw him?"

"Oh, maybe ten, eleven months after we got married. I threw him out one night. Couldn't stand him anymore. Getting divorced was a bitch. You're too young to know, but there wasn't any divorce in New York except for adultery, so I went to Reno, stayed there for six weeks, did it that way. He paid for me to go. He didn't want to do the fake adultery thing, where you set a guy up in a hotel with a woman in a nightgown and the detective comes in and finds them. So there was no other way."

"Did you keep in touch after that?"

"What for? I wanted him out of my life, not in it."

I was curious to know whether he had paid her alimony, but I didn't want to ask. She had mentioned working, so maybe she didn't ask for financial help. "Then you never saw him again?"

"Never."

"Did you talk to him?"

"What about? We went our separate ways."

I really had only one question left and it was the most important one. "I understand Willard was shot back in the 1940s."

"Who told you that?"

"Actually, it came out in the autopsy."

"Oh, yeah, you said he was murdered. Yeah, he was shot." She smiled a little.

"Can you tell me who shot him?"

"Hah! Can I tell you. Bullet missed by a mile, didn't it?"

So she knew about it. I leaned forward. "Who shot him, Mrs. Chester?"

"You'd like to know, wouldn't you?"

"Very much."

"Why? What difference does it make fifty years later?"

"It could be important."

"To you? Who are you, anyway?"

"I'm trying to find out who murdered Willard Platt. His family asked me to help."

"So you think the person who shot him back in the Forties is the same one who killed him last week?"

"I don't think that. I just think it's an unanswered question."

She narrowed her eyes. "What's it worth to you?"

"Excuse me?"

"To find out? How much are you willing to pay if I tell you who shot Willard?"

I was taken aback by her question. It had never occurred to me that she would want to be paid. I had never paid anyone for any information and I wasn't about to start now. "I won't pay anything. I thought you would tell me, since you seem to know."

"I don't seem to know. I know. And I don't have to tell you if I don't want to. Any other questions?"

"I think that was my last one," I said. I took a slip of paper out of my bag and wrote my name and phone number on it. I put it on the round table next to her chair. "If you decide to tell me, you can call collect. I'd really like to know."

She smiled at me, the red lips almost clownlike. "Forget it," she said. "You want to know, make me an offer."

"Thank you for your time. I hope you're feeling better."

"There's no feeling better anymore. There's just getting through the day and hoping there's another one tomorrow."

I didn't say anything, but I felt very sorry for her. I took my coat from the chair where I had left it and went to the door. "Goodbye," I called.

There was no answer.

"Well that's an interesting turn of events," Jack said. "She knows and won't tell. Well why not? People sell everything, why not information?"

"She's a strange woman, Jack. I can just see her as a young, provocative girl. It's as though she never outgrew the part. The makeup she wears is like a caricature. If she washed her face and put a little soft color on it, she'd look almost healthy. But I can tell you for sure she didn't kill Willard Platt, even if she tried a long time ago."

"You think she's the one?"

"I think there's a very good chance."

"So where do you go from here?"

That was the question. I had gone further than I had expected, having found Amelia, but she seemed like a dead end now. I wasn't going to pay her and she had no reason to tell me what I wanted to know unless I did. I had talked to the mayor, who had lied to me, to Mrs. Platt, who may have lied, to Toni, who knew nothing because she wasn't here when her father was murdered, to the owner of the nursery, who wasn't sorry to see Willard dead but didn't strike me as a suspect.

"I guess I should call Joseph," I said. "When I hit a

stone wall, she's always the one who points me in the right direction."

Joseph is Sister Joseph, the General Superior of St. Stephen's, where I lived for fifteen years, many of them as a nun. In addition to being my spiritual director, she is my closest friend. These are not the reasons I go to her when I need help solving a murder. I go because she has a unique way of looking at facts. By the time I ask for her help, I am often so personally involved that it's hard to be objective. Also, in telling her the facts of the case, I often begin to see things myself that had become obscured.

"Go to it," Jack said.

And I did.

I arranged with Joseph that I would drive up tomorrow after mass. While I was on the phone with her, Jack called to say that he'd like to come along; he hadn't been up there for a while. There would probably be plenty of people on the convent grounds, mostly women, as the college was in session, and I wouldn't need a lot of time, perhaps an hour with Joseph. Eddie was a regular on my visits. The nuns all loved him, and I was sure there would be plenty of baking activity in the kitchen when word got around that we were coming.

Eddie had taken a nap while I was gone, and Jack was getting dinner ready when I got off the phone. I asked Jack if it was OK if I went out for a while and he said he didn't mind; he was busy and Eddie would help him. I got in the car and drove over to the apartments where Roger Platt lived.

I decided there was no other way to find him than knocking on doors. First I went through the names on the mailboxes, but nothing looked like a clever permutation of the letters in his name. Nor was there any business name listed. So I went over to the section I had seen him enter last weekend and rang the first bell on the first floor.

I had no success on the first and second floors. Half the apartments had no one home, and I made a note of which ones they were, in case I had to come back on Monday. Where I was able to talk to someone, there was no Roger and they had never heard of him. I was starting to feel that this was a wild goose chase—I've had many of them in recent years—when I pressed a button for the fifteenth or so time. I heard footsteps coming toward the door, then the bolt turned and the door was pulled open.

And I stood face-to-face with Doris Platt.

16

I don't know which of us was more surprised. We looked at each other for several seconds, neither of us speaking. Finally she said, "You'd better come in."

I went inside and into the living room, where a tall man in his forties rose from where he had been sitting.

"I'm Roger Platt," he said. And to my surprise, he offered me his hand.

I shook it and said, "I've been looking for you."

"I gather as much. Why don't you sit down? You're Mrs. Brooks, I assume."

"Yes. Chris. I'm glad you're all right."

"Why wouldn't I be?"

"No one's seen you for a while. Your mother was worried."

"I know. Doris tells me you followed me home one night."

"I did. But I didn't know which apartment you lived in. I've been knocking on doors."

"That's what I did," Doris said. "But I started on the top floor because I knew Roger wouldn't want to be anywhere else."

Interesting, I thought. So nobody in the building got

visits from both of us. "I hope you'll call your mother," I said to him.

"I will. Is there anything else?" He seemed anxious to dismiss me.

"Yes, there is. I have a few questions."

In that moment, I decided to find out what he knew of his father's past, even if it meant unsettling him. He had done enough unsettling himself to deserve it. "Did you know about your father's first marriage?"

"My father's *what*?"

"I've just come back from talking to your father's first wife. I just wondered whether you knew about her."

"Mrs. Brooks, you've got a few lines crossed. My father married my mother after the war and that's the only marriage he ever had."

"You're wrong about that. A lawyer friend of mine dug up the marriage certificate yesterday and I was able to trace her. We spoke this afternoon."

"This is crazy. Next you'll tell me he had kids with her."

"He didn't. They weren't married very long, about a year. I don't know whether your mother is aware of her existence."

"Do *not* discuss this with my mother," he ordered.

"I don't intend to. Mr. Platt, are you aware that your father was shot back in the Forties?"

"Doris was just telling me about the autopsy. I'm starting to wonder if I know who my father was."

"I have a strong feeling that it may have been his first wife who shot him, but I don't know that for certain. She knows who did it, or at least she claims to, but she won't tell me." I didn't think the details of our conversation needed to be revealed.

"I'm finding all this hard to believe. Why don't the police know this?"

"It's possible that they do. They certainly know the results of the autopsy. But police don't usually look too far back in time for motives or possible killers. I find that everything that happens in a life can be relevant."

"I hear you talked to Dad's old friend, Harry."

"I did. He knew about your father's first marriage. He was a witness."

Roger shook his head. "I can't believe this."

"He also knew your father had been shot."

"You're not going to suggest that Harry killed Dad."

"I'm not suggesting anything. But that seems unlikely. He would have had to come out here on Saturday and somehow get back. Does he own a car?"

"Not that I know of. I'm not sure he ever did."

"Can you tell me why you weren't at the funeral?" I asked.

"I can, but I'm not going to. How I conduct my life is my business."

"I heard that there were bad feelings between your father and Mr. Vitale at the nursery across the road."

"There were. I'm sure part of that was my father's fault. He was never an easy person to get along with. But don't believe everything you hear. If my father drove a hard bargain, you can be sure Vitale did too. I think in the back of Vitale's mind was that he would develop the land he wanted to buy from us."

"You mean build houses?"

"Exactly. And they would have gone for a fortune. That

area has everything—privacy, a view, no traffic. It's an ideal place to live."

Those were interesting thoughts. It had never occurred to me that the nursery wanted anything but the right to plant trees and shrubs. Perhaps Willard Platt had demanded a promise in writing that the land would not be developed and Mr. Vitale refused to give it. It was possible that both parties had acted in a less than ethical manner. "I've been getting the story in bits and pieces," I said. "I see that there's more to it than I originally thought."

"There's more to everything," Roger said without elucidating.

"Is there a way I can reach you if I have any more questions?"

"No there isn't. I don't want you coming here and I don't want you calling me. Doris and I are in touch and she can pass along a message, but don't expect me to respond. The truth is, I don't care very much."

"You had a bad relationship with him," I said.

"I had no relationship with him. I didn't like him and he didn't care very much for me. At some time in my life I decided I was tired of being a disappointment to him, so I stopped seeing very much of him. It's made my life a lot easier."

I wondered if he felt the same way about his wife. "Thanks for your time," I said, standing.

Doris walked me to the door and went outside into the hall. "I just wanted you to know, I found Roger about an hour before you got here."

"Today?"

"Yes. You had told me where you saw him so I came

over and started ringing bells. He answered the door. He was very surprised to see me. I don't know if he'll move because of this."

"Then you're not thinking of getting back together."

"We haven't discussed it. I found him, Chris. I didn't make a change in our lives."

"OK. Thanks for telling me."

"And I can assure you, Roger never knew that his father had a first wife. I was watching him when you told him. You really shook him up."

I had had the same feeling. "I wonder if Winnie knows," I said.

"Please don't say anything. This has been so hard on her. Don't make things worse."

"I won't."

I guess one of the things I like best about trying to solve a homicide is the way facts surface one by one and little by little. You think you have a clear picture and then something else turns up and the picture is no longer clear. The incident involving the land was a good example. If what Roger had just told me was true, there was certainly bad faith on both sides. And I was now inclined toward Willard Platt's side. I didn't blame him at all for wanting to keep the land on the hill from being developed. And if he changed his mind, why shouldn't he have been the one to benefit financially? He could have sold off some of the land to a developer, who would surely pay considerably more than a nursery that presumably wanted it for trees and flowers. No one in this whole mess was completely clean.

Jack and I had a lot to talk about that evening. "Do you

believe Doris Platt when she said she had just found her husband?" he asked.

"I think I do, but I could be wrong. She certainly took pains to tell me exactly how and when she found him and that she started on the third floor, which meant the people I talked to hadn't also talked to her."

"So now she knows where he's living. You think he'll bolt again? Find another place to live so she can't find him?"

"I think he may. Unless he changes his mind and decides to give the marriage another chance."

"I don't know why he'd do that. He probably sees just enough of his family to suit him. But the land thing is intriguing, Chris. I have a feeling Roger may have told you more of the truth than anyone else."

"I agree. And it's changed my feelings about Mr. Vitale. I really saw him as the victim in all this. But if he refused to promise not to develop the land, well, he's just as duplicitous as everyone else I've talked to."

"I think you're right."

I smiled. "Right or wrong, it's always interesting."

It became even more interesting later that evening. We were just getting ready to go upstairs to bed when the phone rang. It was after ten-thirty and the sound of the ring scared me a little. We don't get many late night calls.

"Chris, it's Toni. I'm sorry to bother you at this hour but I'm leaving tomorrow and I wanted to catch you while I could."

"Is everything all right?"

"I don't even know how to answer that question anymore. We've found something and it's quite disturbing."

I pulled a chair over. "Go on."

"We suddenly realized over dinner that we hadn't looked for Dad's will. He wrote it so long ago that Mom couldn't remember who the lawyer was, but she was sure there was a copy in the house. We found it." She stopped.

"Is there a problem?"

"I don't know how to say this. Dad wrote a will years ago and put it away. He told my mother that he was cutting Roger out because—well, because they didn't get along and Roger refused to toe the line. I think we've talked about this."

"Yes."

"Well, we found it in the file drawer where Mom knew he kept it. It was exactly what she expected. Everything is left to her, and on her death it all goes to me and to the grandchildren."

"Then what's the problem? It seems to me that a will cutting Roger off shows there isn't much motive for him to have murdered your father. He was aware of the terms of the will, wasn't he?"

"Oh, yes. Dad saw to it that he knew. The problem is—Chris, there's another will in the drawer, a newer one."

"I see." I waited, wondering what she was going to spring on me.

"It was also written several years ago, but it's much newer. It still leaves everything to Mom during her lifetime, but on her death, it's divided evenly between Roger and me."

I was stunned. I had spent half an hour listening to this man talk about his unpleasant feelings about his father. "Do you have any idea why he might have changed it?" I asked.

"None. And Mom didn't know anything about it either."

"Amazing. Does Roger know about it?"

"I don't know. I haven't called and I don't think I want to. In fact, I really don't want to tell anybody. Is that OK?"

That was probably the reason she was calling. She didn't want to tell the police for obvious reasons. "I don't think you have to tell anyone unless you're asked by the police. Then you'll have to be truthful."

"I will be. I just hope they don't ask."

She gave me her number at home in case there was anything I had to talk to her about, and I wished her a good trip.

Then I told Jack what I had learned.

"And she has no idea why Platt changed his mind?" he said.

"No."

"But he's got to know—Roger, I mean."

"I can't get in touch with him, Jack. I don't have his cell number, he's not listed anywhere, and I don't even know where he works. Doris isn't going to help. If she does, he'll just take his anger out on her."

"Well, maybe the old man just had a change of heart. It happens, you know. You get older, family becomes more important. You know the drill."

"But they didn't get back together. Roger didn't like him. He said so very plainly."

Jack shrugged. "Ask Sister Joseph. She's the one with all the insights."

17

We got an early start Sunday morning after mass. I was so used to driving myself that it seemed strange to be on the passenger side of the car. It was a beautiful day, sunny and on the warm side for a change. There was talk of April showers, but not for a few days. Since we'd had plenty of snow earlier in the year, I was happy to do with less rain.

We arrived before noon and greeted all my old friends as we walked in to the Mother House. They had arranged for Jack and Eddie to have lunch with a few of the nuns while I was upstairs eating off a tray in Sister Joseph's office. Naturally, there were cookies for Eddie as soon as we arrived, but I didn't worry about whether he would eat well or overdo the sweets. We didn't make the trip all that often and I wanted this place to be as dear to him as it was to me.

Joseph came down to say hello and marvel at Eddie. He had reached a point in his development where he could carry on a conversation, and that was very important to her. It created the kind of bond that just oohing and aahing over a cute little child could not make. We left them in the care of the nuns, and Joseph and I went upstairs and down the hall to her office.

"I almost have the feeling your son may answer the telephone next time I call and tell me how his mom and dad are doing," she said as we settled ourselves at the long table.

"That may happen soon. He's actually picked the phone up once or twice but he doesn't quite know what to do when he hears a strange voice."

"Well, progress is wonderful and I'm glad to see you all looking so good. I gather you have a ticklish murder you're trying to solve."

"A murder in which everyone seems to be lying or withholding the truth."

"Then it will be a challenge. Let's begin."

And like an ancient ritual, I narrated my tale, starting with the embarrassing event on April Fools' Day and finishing with my conversations with Roger Platt yesterday afternoon and then his sister at night. As always, Joseph sat across from me with a pile of unlined paper in front of her and several well-sharpened pencils within reach. She wrote frequently but hardly interjected a question. When I was finished, she started back through her notes.

"Amazing that Arnold was able to get you that very important piece of information," she said first. She had met Arnold when Jack and I were married and they admire each other greatly.

"It was actually Arnold's intern who did the research, and he wasn't particularly happy that she dug out my information before she worked on the client he's representing."

"Well, it whetted her appetite for the paying customer. And how fortunate, in a country where everyone seems to move all the time, that this woman's sister stayed put for half a century."

"Very fortunate. But I have no hope that Amelia will tell me who shot Willard. And I will not pay her for the information."

"I agree," Joseph said. "I don't like the taint of money either. But you might call during the week to inquire about her health. That might dispose her to be kind to you."

"I'll do that, but I almost hate to ask her. She looks very ill and very weak. I have a feeling she'll go to sleep one night with her secret and not wake up in the morning."

"Is it your feeling that she pulled the trigger?"

"Yes. But it's only a feeling."

"Is it also your feeling that Willard Platt carried a weapon with him every day of his life because he feared for his life?"

"I think maybe he did at thc beginning, after he was shot. Later, it became something of a game. He was the man with the cane. It distinguished him from other men. He was an actor at heart. This was a role he played for the rest of his life, a role he enjoyed playing."

"That does sound reasonable." Joseph made marks next to some of her notes. "You've established that the wife was home when Willard was murdered?"

"She admitted it. She didn't try to hide it at all. It would be difficult to hide. She didn't drive. Unless someone picked her up and brought her back, where else could she be?"

"Does she know that you suspect her?"

"Jack is the one who thinks she's a strong suspect. I can't bring myself to feel that way, but everything he says is very reasonable. But no, she doesn't know. I haven't said a word to anyone."

"And now that her husband is dead, she's driving again."

"Apparently, she's kept up her license all these years."

"I find that interesting," Joseph said. "She stopped driving because she was involved in a terrible accident, but she kept renewing the license."

"It's not very hard. It comes in the mail, you fill it out, you send a check. Why wouldn't she?"

"Having that license certainly makes her life much easier now. From the way you've described where she lives, she'd be in a real pickle without a car. It's almost as though she were waiting for this moment."

"I know it looks that way." It saddened me to think that Winnie could have planned this murder for so long.

"The nursery land deal is also very interesting. It gives Mr. Vitale a motive for murder, but having killed Willard Platt, what does he get out of it?"

"Just a feeling of revenge, I guess," I said. "There's no way he'll ever be able to buy that land. If Winnie needs money, I expect she'll sell it to the highest bidder."

"And there will be bidders," Joseph said. "I see what they're building around here, and the size of the houses and the prices they're asking are almost unbelievable."

They would get those outrageous prices in Oakwood, of that I was sure. "So where does that leave me?" I asked. "Roger is still the one I think had the greatest grievance against his father. He endured years of what today would be called psychological abuse. His father cut him out of his will because, in his eyes, Roger wasn't a good son. And now we find that the father secretly changed his will so that this son that he never got along with inherits as much as the daughter who was the apple of his eye." Toni's phone call had caused me a great deal of soul searching.

I had lain awake for a long time trying to figure out what had prompted Willard to reinstate his son.

"It would be nice to know if Roger knew about the change," Joseph said.

"It's crucial, Joseph. If Roger knew, he had a motive. If Roger didn't know, if Roger thought he didn't benefit financially from his father's death, why would he kill him?"

"There are other things in the world besides money."

I smiled. "Which you and I know well. I don't think Roger knew about his father's change of heart. I think something happened last week and he went to talk to his father and they argued. Roger knew about the canes. He grabbed the one in the garage and killed his father with it in a fit of anger."

"And then pulled the flag on the mailbox down before he left so the mailman might not stop."

"Someone did," I said. "I think it could only be the murderer."

"Chris, tell me again about the accident that killed the child. There's something about it that bothers me."

I went through it again and finished by saying, "There isn't much."

"I think that's what troubles me. Such a terrible thing happens and it's all the fault of a piece of ice and a tree. I suppose I feel that when a child dies, there should be more. The world should quiver. Nothing can be more terrible than that."

"I'll see what I can find," I said, "but I'm not sure where to go for more information."

"You'll find it," she said with the confidence of one who believes anything is possible.

Our lunch arrived just then and we settled into eating and chatting about what was going on in the convent. The college, happily, was thriving, full of young women who wanted an education separate from men, although there were plenty of young men on campus on weekends. But at the convent the number of novices had dwindled to practically nothing and the fate of the convent was no longer certain. There was talk of a merger with another Franciscan convent, but at the moment it was only talk. Since this place was so much a part of me, I could not imagine an influx of new people with their own long history who would want at least some of their ways and habits to be adopted by St. Stephen's.

When we were done, we went downstairs. Jack and Eddie were out walking with a couple of the nuns, so Joseph and I started out on our own walk. We stopped briefly at the chapel where I had prayed as a nun and had been married almost five years ago. There I lit my three candles, for my parents and Aunt Meg, and left a gift in the box.

Three nuns, sitting separately, were deep in prayer or thought. It struck me how old the nuns had begun to look, not just the retired women in the Villa, but the ones actively running St. Stephen's. There were hardly any in their twenties anymore, only a few in their thirties. Joseph herself was about fifty, although to me she always seemed younger, a woman who lived a life according to old customs, but who was knowledgeable about the new and embraced it when it suited the needs of the convent. I felt a kind of fear in my gut, almost a panic. From the way Joseph had spoken, it no longer seemed a question of whether the convent would survive by itself, but when measures would have to be taken to ensure its survival by changing its very nature.

I turned to find Joseph. She was standing in the back, near the door, looking thoughtful, as though she had all the time in the world. When she saw me coming toward her, she smiled and pushed the door open.

"Did you see the young couple sitting in a pew on the right?" she asked.

"I noticed them. Is she a student?"

"A sophomore. I assume that's a boyfriend. He comes frequently on the weekends and they always sit in the same place, holding hands and whispering. There are other places they could sit, places they could be warmer and more comfortable. The cafeteria is open to guests. But they always come here. It's rather a sweet mystery."

"It is sweet," I said.

"Do they talk about religion? I wonder. Or about themselves? Or perhaps some problem they have that they share with no one else."

"Sometimes just being in love is a problem. He's in one place, she's in another. It's nice that they feel comfortable in the chapel."

"Yes it is."

We walked toward the college buildings. A few hardy students were out reading under leafless trees. Others were walking alone or in groups. I listened to the sound of girls' voices, happy voices.

"I hope the convent survives the way it is," I said.

"We all do, but we must be realists."

"That's not easy."

"No, but it's less disappointing than being an optimist in a bad situation."

"I suppose so."

"Don't sound so sad, Chris. I'm working very hard to keep things the way we all want them. Father Kramer is working with me. The bishop is familiar with our needs. We won't give up."

My eyes were full of tears. This place had saved my life. These women had given me a home. This particular woman had helped me make something of myself while letting me believe I had done it on my own. I wanted this place and these people to exist forever.

Near the cafeteria we ran into Jack and Eddie and their escorts. It gave me a lift.

"You're very quiet," Jack said on the way home.

"It's the first time I've ever heard Joseph talking so seriously about whether the convent will survive."

"That bad?"

"There are so few novices. I hate to think what the average age of the nuns is today."

"She have any ideas?"

"Nothing that I like."

He patted my hand. "Eddie and I had a good walk. It's a beautiful place. Kind of makes me feel good just to be there."

That was my point.

18

At home I told Jack what Joseph and I had discussed. I didn't know how to find information on the fatal accident Winnie had been involved in without going through police files. There are local newspapers where we live, but they are not the quality of the major papers in the metropolitan area. Besides being poorly written and copyedited, they have little of the kind of information I was looking for.

Jack called the police station. He has a very good relationship with the Oakwood police force. One or two of the cops have become good acquaintances and keep him posted when he needs to know something.

But after he asked if he could see the file on the Platt accident, I was aware from the way he spoke that he had been turned down.

"Could you tell me who was first on the scene?" he asked. He had a pen in his hand. "Uh-huh. Yeah, I see. Any detectives involved?" He wrote something and thanked whomever he was talking to.

"Boy, they're tight on this one."

"He won't let you see the file?"

"He gave me a song and dance about a child being

involved. I don't know if he was making it up as he went along or whether they've gotten the word from the commissioner—"

"Or the mayor," I suggested.

"Yeah, right. It could be the mayor. Anyway, he gave me a couple of names and he's probably on the phone right now telling these guys not to open their mouths to me."

"I don't understand it. It was an accident that involved only one car, so there wasn't any lawsuit. What could be the problem?"

"You know, I think this is the first time I've ever asked to see a file. It's possible they just don't like letting anyone outside the department look at them. In the past, I've asked when an autopsy took place, what the results were, that kind of thing. So let's see if I can find out what's going on from the cop on the scene and the detective who followed up. You'll be glad to know you already know the detective." He gave me a grin.

"I do?"

"The one you got on with so well when that homicide happened last Mother's Day."

"Oh *that* one." I'd had my problems with Detective Joe Fox, but we ended up working together when I led him to a killer. "You talk to him, OK?"

"Sure. Let me wait till tomorrow morning when everyone's back at work. Including me."

On Monday morning I went out with Eddie after breakfast, getting back about ten-thirty. I decided that was late enough that Amelia Chester would be awake. I called her number and waited for many rings until she answered, her voice so weak I could barely hear her.

"Mrs. Chester, this is Chris Bennett. We talked on Saturday."

"Chris. Yes."

She sounded really bad and I wondered if I should call her sister and tell her. "I just wanted to know how you're feeling."

I heard her take a couple of breaths. "Not very good today."

"I'm sorry." I felt terrible. "Is there anything I can do?"

"Let me get back into bed."

"I apologize. I didn't know you were sleeping."

"I wasn't." She hung up.

I knew as I put the phone down that there was no hope, either for her or for my desire to get the information that I needed. I sat thinking about this old, sick woman, alone in her apartment. Before I could think about what to do, the phone rang.

I grabbed it, hoping it was Amelia. To my surprise, it was Winnie Platt.

"Chris," she said. "I have a favor to ask you."

"Sure. What is it?"

"Could you come up here and help me practice my driving for half an hour?"

"I'll be there. Eddie is with me. Is that all right?"

"I'd love to see him."

Eddie was happy to visit her. He liked the house and he liked her. I told him we would sit in her car while she practiced driving but I think that left him confused. Older people knew how to drive.

When we got there, I transferred our child's seat to the

back of her car and got Eddie in it. Then I sat next to Winnie as she took the wheel.

"It's such a big car," she said. "Will always liked them big but I didn't. I feel like I'm the captain of a battleship."

"You'll get over it. When you see how easily you can move it, you won't think about the size."

She backed out of the driveway somewhat unsteadily, but it was a wide driveway and she stayed off the lawn. Then, to my surprise, she headed down the hill.

"Oh, you're going to Oakwood Avenue?" I said.

"Yes, didn't I tell you?"

"Sorry. I thought you were just going to drive up and down the hill here."

"I did that with Toni. I want to try real traffic with you next to me before I go out alone."

"You're doing fine," I said.

She got down to the bottom of the hill, stopped smoothly, put her turn signal on, and turned right. I knew we would pass the place where the accident had occurred, and maybe that was what she wanted to do, prove to herself that she could do it. She kept the speed down to twenty-five miles an hour, hardly touching the accelerator, although the limit was forty, and two cars passed her, the driver of one giving her a nasty look. It didn't seem to faze her. She looked straight ahead, her hands gripping the wheel rather tightly.

"You're doing well, Winnie," I said. "Absolutely fine."

"Thank you. Roger's house is down that way." She let go of the wheel for a second and pointed with her left hand. "Remember?"

We kept going and at some point I realized we had passed the site of the accident. "Just fine," I said.

"It really comes back, doesn't it?"

"You're a good driver, Winnie."

"Yes, I feel better now." She kept going, and I wondered if she had a destination in mind or if she was just looking for a place to turn around, but it didn't matter. I knew it was important for her to do this, and I had plenty of time.

"I'm taking you both to lunch," she said, her face relaxing into a smile.

"Lunch!" Eddie said excitedly from the backseat.

"Yes, Eddie, I'm taking you and your mommy to lunch. Do you like to eat in restaurants?"

"I want pizza," Eddie said ungraciously.

"You'll get something nice," I assured him.

"He's very sweet," she said generously. "We'll have a nice lunch, Eddie." She was much more at ease, and I realized she had risen to thc challenge. It was the first time she had been behind the wheel at that place since the accident. She knew now that she could do it. I felt a great admiration for this woman. The worst possible thing had happened to her, something that surely haunted her awake and asleep, but she knew now she had overcome it enough to be independent once more.

"Do you want to turn around and go in the other direction?" I asked her.

"I don't think so. I've done what I wanted to. You've heard about it, haven't you?"

"Yes."

"Even with Will driving, I always shut my eyes when we reached that place. But I knew if I was going to be able to get my own groceries and take my clothes to the cleaner, I had to overcome that."

"You did very well."

"Yes, I did well." She smiled. "How's the Oakwood Diner?" she asked. "I don't know if Eddie can get what he wants there, but there's lots of good food and they'll wrap up what's left so you can eat the leftovers at home."

"That sounds good."

"Do you need anything at Prince's?" she asked, as though she had such control over her life that she could deviate from a plan with no untoward consequences.

"Thanks, we're fine. But if you want to stop for yourself—"

"No. Toni saw to it that I have enough in the house to keep me going for a week at least. But I can go there anytime I want now."

She drove past Prince's parking lot and Eddie pointed to it and called out its name. I guess he knew it so well because he sometimes got a cookie as a present when we shopped there.

"You're a smart boy, Eddie," Winnie said. "We're going to have lunch at the diner. Do you know the diner too?"

"No," he said. "What's the diner?"

"You'll see."

I told Winnie that I didn't take him out for lunch very often and she said good, it would be a new experience for him. She pulled into their parking lot and we all got out. Inside, they gave Eddie a booster seat and we sat opposite Winnie and went through the enormous menu.

After we had ordered, Winnie said, "Toni told you about the will, didn't she?"

"Yes. She called Saturday night. I take it you didn't know anything about the second one."

"I had no idea. It was such a shock, such a happy surprise, really. I had thought Roger would inherit nothing of Will's money."

"I gather they didn't get along very well."

"It was awful. This was my wonderful son, so bright and so mixed up. Will and I argued about how he treated Roger, but Will was a stubborn man. His son had to do what his father wanted him to do. It never seemed to make a difference that Roger did what he liked, was a happy man, had a wonderful family, and was successful at his work.

"Toni, on the other hand, could do no wrong. Not that she ever did anything wrong; it's just that Will forgave everything. When he wrote his will all those years ago and left everything to Toni after my death, I was heartsick."

"I can understand that."

"And then he changed the will and never told me."

Our food came and I got Eddie started, hoping he wouldn't make a mess and knowing he probably would. Winnie had been right about the size of the portions. They were huge. Eddie and I would have lunch another time with our leftovers.

"Did your husband's relationship to Roger change in the last few years?" I asked. "After that second will was written?"

"Not that I noticed. It's as though he separated the money from his feelings. Although I have to say that by this time, Roger was the one that didn't want a relationship with his father. He'd struggled for so long and lost, I think he just gave up."

"Have the police said anything about their investigation?" I asked.

"Nothing. They've been to the house more times than

I can count. They took a million pictures of the garage, then a lot more when we found the missing cane. They asked the same questions over and over. How did the cane get there? Who has a key to the house? Why did it take you so long to find it? It's as if they're waiting for someone to make a mistake and tell them what they're hoping to hear. But there's no mistake. Someone came and killed my husband and I don't know who it was."

"If someone had taken the cane and shoved it through the opening in the basement window, how would he have gotten from the garage to that window?"

"He would have had to go to the back of the house. He could have done it two ways, around the garage or across the front and then around the other side of the house."

"Where you were sitting that afternoon, would you have seen someone go across the back of the house?"

"I'm sure I would have," she said. "It's all glass back there. You've seen it. How could anyone walk in front of those picture windows and sliding doors without my seeing him?"

That, of course, was exactly my question. "But if he took a chance and went across the front of the house, then he could have pushed the cane into the basement without you seeing him."

"But the mailman could have seen him if he was driving by. Did anyone talk to the mailman?"

"I did," I said. "I don't know if the police did."

"The police think my son did this," Winnie said sadly. "He didn't. He may not have gotten along with his father, but he's not a killer. Why would he do such a thing? It isn't logical."

I had felt the same way when I knew that Roger stood

to inherit nothing. "Could Roger have known about the new will?" I asked softly.

"If I didn't know, nobody knew." She said it with a note of defiance.

"Did the same lawyer draw up both wills?" I asked.

"It doesn't look that way. There's a business card clipped on the new will with a name I've never heard of. Maybe the other lawyer died."

Or Willard decided to start with a clean slate, hiring someone who didn't know the history of his relationship with his son. I wanted to ask her if she knew about Willard's first marriage, but I couldn't bring myself to do it. I thought the chances of her knowing about it were fifty-fifty, but I didn't want to be the one to let her know.

She started talking to Eddie at that point, and I decided not to pursue any of the unanswered questions I still had. When we finished eating, we left with three doggie bags. On the way back, Winnie drove with more confidence, but still at a slow speed. I had the feeling she would work on that too.

Eddie took a nap and Jack called while I was finishing up my papers for my class the next day.

"OK, talked to Joe Fox. He remembers that accident investigation very well, mostly because there was a child involved. He said the boy was killed instantly."

"Was Winnie hurt very much?"

"Cuts and bruises. But she was completely traumatized, could hardly talk. Joe said he really felt for her."

"Any chance there was another car involved?" I asked.

"Not from what he said. He figures she was driving too fast for the condition of the road. She began to use the brake and the car went into a skid she couldn't pull out of. He said the skid marks on the road were a real clincher. They helped him reconstruct the path of the car right into the tree. And by the way, no one ever told him not to discuss the case. He's with the county so that doesn't surprise me. And I heard about the cane."

"What about it?"

"There are prints, or at least partials, all over it: Willard's, Winnie's—"

"They took Winnie's prints?"

"They had to. You have to exclude prints when you're looking for a killer's. So they had hers. But finding her prints on the cane really doesn't mean very much. She probably touched it when it was in her way. The top of the cane had been wiped fairly clean."

"So the killer thought about that. Do the police know there's a housekeeper who comes to clean? She probably dusts the canes and polishes the metal tops."

"I gotta believe they know what they're doing, Chris. Although they're grudgingly grateful that you brought the cane up in the first place. Also the stuff about Platt's legs. They're pretty sure he walked just fine without a cane, that he carried one for effect. You call his first wife back today?"

"I did." I told him what had happened and that I felt she was very ill. "I don't expect I'll be talking to her again. I hope her sister knows how bad her condition is."

"So I guess that's a secret that'll stay with her. Look, what do you say I ask Joe Fox over for tonight? He sounded willing and he could bring the file on the accident."

"That's fine. I'll pick up something to munch on with coffee."

"Gee, we could have him over every night."

"We'd get fat as pigs."

"Well, I tried. By the way, I haven't been able to get hold of the cop who was first on the scene at the accident, but I'm still trying."

I didn't think he'd have much luck but I had an idea of my own.

19

It was a simple idea. Later in the afternoon, I took Eddie and went out to buy a cake that I could serve in the evening. On the way home I stopped at the corner of Oakwood and a street with a lot of houses. The accident had happened right near that corner. I pulled into the driveway of the house I thought was the closest to that spot and rang the doorbell. When the woman inside opened the door, I recognized her from church.

"You're Chris Brooks," she said.

"Yes, and this is my son, Eddie. I think you're Carolyn."

"Yes, Carolyn Haney. Come on in."

She was about my age and had a couple of kids who came down to see who the visitor was. In a minute Eddie had been whisked away upstairs.

"I wanted to ask you about the accident a few years ago in which the little boy was killed."

"The Platt boy. I get a chill when I think of it. It happened right across the street. I heard the crash. You never forget a sound like that."

"So you were home."

"I was right here in the kitchen cooking dinner. I heard the sound but I had something on the stove and I couldn't leave right away. When I could, I went to the dining room window and looked out. I couldn't see anything from there so I went into the living room. It was dark out and the weather was terrible. I could sort of see the lights from the back of the car and then the doorbell rang. It was Mrs. Platt. She was almost hysterical, crying and saying, 'Help me, help me. I need an ambulance.' She said something about her grandson. I told her to come in but she said she couldn't leave him and she went out again. I called the police and said there'd been an accident, and when I gave them the address, they said they knew about it and they were on their way. I heard the sirens after I hung up."

"So someone else called first."

"I don't know who, but there are a lot of houses around here. Someone probably heard the crash and called right away."

"Did you go out to the car?"

"Oh yes. I grabbed my coat and my keys and called upstairs to the kids to stay put. It was a terrible night, cold and snowy. I dashed over and got just a quick look at the boy. It was terrible." Her eyes filled. "It's hard to think about it," she said. "He was just a child."

"Was anyone else there when you went out?"

"People were stopping their cars, people were coming out of their houses. It was a real mess when the ambulance and police cars got there."

"Was the boy alive?" I asked.

She shook her head. "I don't think so."

"What about Mrs. Platt? Was she hurt?"

"Nothing that I could see. If you saw how the car hit the tree, you'd understand. The tree went right through the passenger side. He never had a chance. But the other side of the car didn't look that bad. I'm sure the alignment was all off, but it was really just the passenger side that suffered."

"Did you stay long?"

"I couldn't. I asked Mrs. Platt if she'd like a cup of tea or to come inside but she turned me down. Then I saw my kids coming out and I didn't want them to see what happened, so I went back inside. Can I ask why you're interested in this?"

"I'm trying to figure out who murdered Willard Platt," I said. "I just wanted to know more about the accident."

"There can't be any connection, it happened so long ago. The boy was their grandson. I think Mrs. Platt was driving him home from Boy Scouts or something."

"You didn't see any other car that could have been involved in the accident?"

"A second car? No. And she never said anything about a second car. It was snowing and there were icy patches on the road. She was probably driving too fast."

Which might account for how slowly she had driven us this morning. "Thanks, Carolyn," I said, getting up.

"Did I help?" she asked with a smile.

"Not really. I keep learning new things but they don't fit together. Yet."

"Well, you could ask Fran Goldman across Oakwood Avenue. I saw her at the car that night. Maybe she saw something."

I said I would, but not today. I retrieved Eddie with some difficulty and we drove home.

"It was Officer Malcolm who was first on the scene," Jack said over dinner. We knew Officer Malcolm. He was a young man and must have been fairly new on the police force when the accident happened. "It really shook him up."

"I can imagine."

"He said Mrs. P was falling apart, but she didn't seem to be hurt beyond some cuts."

"What about the boy?"

"Looked very bad. They needed the jaws of life to get him out, and by that time he was gone."

"What a horror."

"Yeah."

I got Eddie off to bed before Detective Joe Fox arrived. It was the first time I'd seen him since our somewhat contentious relationship the year before. This time he was not only in a good mood, he brought me a small bunch of flowers.

Jack had a fire going and we sat and gabbed a bit before Joe Fox patted the file on the sofa next to him and asked what I wanted to know.

I told him what was going on, and he said he didn't think the accident could have played any part in the current homicide. It appeared to be a one-car accident that happened the way Mrs. Platt had described it. "The only broken glass came from the car she was driving," he said.

"And I guess if there'd been paint scrapes you would have seen it."

"You bet I would. Good cup of coffee, Mrs. Brooks."

"Thank you." I glanced at Jack, who had made the coffee.

Joe Fox opened the file jacket and looked through several sheets of paper. "She was properly licensed, she was wearing the required glasses, the car was registered to her, it looked to be in good condition. Why would you think this has anything to do with the homicide of her husband five or six years later?"

"Actually, it was Sister Joseph's idea. You remember Sister Joseph?"

"I do indeed. Fine lady. I gave her a hard time, as I remember, which she didn't deserve."

"I'll tell her you said that."

"I'm not involved in the current homicide investigation," he said, "but it sounds like an interesting case, a man killed with his own weapon."

"A cane that held a two-edged blade."

"And the scuttlebutt is he didn't need a cane. Is that true?"

"Apparently."

"Just liked to walk around with a deadly weapon, I guess."

"He'd been shot when he was a young man," Jack said. "Just after the war. Chris thinks he may have been afraid that the shooter might come back and get him."

"This is fifty years later. The shooter's probably dead and buried by now. Wild story." He looked at the blazing fire thoughtfully. Then he turned to me. "If there's something you know about this homicide that you'd like to tell the police," he said, "you can tell me and I'll let them know."

There were things I knew but nothing I wanted to tell the police at that point. "I don't think so," I said.

"It's over a week, Mrs. Brooks. From what I've heard, there's someone they like for this, but they don't have anything concrete."

"I don't know who did it. If I figure it out, you can be sure I won't keep it to myself. I told you what I knew, didn't I?"

"You certainly did. And you didn't even brag about how much more you uncovered than I did."

I smiled and offered him another piece of cake, which he accepted. That was the end of our conversation about the accident. There was nothing I wanted to tell him and not much more he could tell us. As I had heard, no charges were ever pressed against Winnie for the accident. What she suffered was self-inflicted, and it was a life sentence.

After Joe Fox left, we cleaned up the dishes, watched some late news, and went upstairs. As I was getting ready for bed the phone rang, giving me an uneasy feeling.

"This is Maureen Benzinger," the voice said. "Is this Chris Bennett?"

"Yes it is. Is something wrong, Mrs. Benzinger?"

"Everything's wrong. My sister was taken to the hospital this afternoon." A sob escaped her. "She's in very bad shape. I don't think she'll make it this time."

"I'm terribly sorry."

"She asked to see you."

"What?"

"She said she wants to see you. Can you come tomorrow?"

"I don't know," I said. "I teach in the morning."

"Well, if you don't get there soon, she won't be there anymore. It's Jacoby Hospital in the Bronx. It's not too far from Amelia's apartment."

"I can find it," I said, meaning that Jack would tell me how to get there.

"Come soon." She hung up.

I stood with the phone in my hand till Jack asked what was the matter. I told him.

"She wants to get it off her chest."

"I guess so." I hung up the phone, which was making annoying noises. "I'll drive down after my class. Can you route me to Jacoby Hospital?"

"No problem. Here's what you do. . . ."

20

I took my leftover lunch from Monday to the college, grabbed a bottle of cold juice, and stuffed my lunch in my mouth the minute my class was over, apologizing that I could not stay to answer questions. I try to be available, especially right after class, as I don't rate an office, but I was literally fighting against time. For all I knew, Amelia had passed from the earth overnight, but I had to make the effort.

And it was truly an effort. I felt queasy just thinking about what was in store for me. Amelia Chester had looked so bad when I'd seen her on Saturday, I didn't want to have to look at her in worse condition. Still, this was almost a dying wish, and I had to respect it.

I was down at the hospital before two, my lunch sitting uncomfortably in my stomach. I found my way to the desk and was told someone was in Mrs. Chester's room, but I could go up. I assumed the visitor was her sister.

I gathered myself together before I reached the door, knocked, and walked in. An old woman sat in a chair looking tired and worn. A thin pale figure lay on the bed, the head raised slightly.

The woman in the chair got up and looked at me. "Are you Miss Bennett?"

"Yes," I said softly. "Mrs. Benzinger?"

She nodded. "I'm her sister. She's sleeping. I don't know if she'll wake up."

"Did she give you a message for me?"

"She just said to call you. Said she wanted to tell you something." She walked over to the bed and put her hand on the pale white hand that lay on the cover. "Amelia? Amelia, dear, someone's here to see you."

A shudder ran through Amelia's upper body but her eyes remained closed. Whatever makeup she might have been wearing when she was taken to the hospital had been washed off, leaving her face as pale as her hand. A little red color still marked her lips like the memory of a better time. On the far side of the bed a clear fluid dripped from a bag to a tube and into her other hand. I stood away from the bed and watched, sensing I was too late, understanding the meaning of the phrase: "She took the secret to her grave."

Mrs. Benzinger brushed her sister's forehead and patted her hand. Amelia did not move. "She's come to see you, dear. Chris has come to see you. You asked for her, remember?" When there was no response, she turned around and shook her head.

"I'm so sorry," I said. "Can I get you something to eat or drink? There must be a cafeteria."

"Yes, downstairs. I could use a cup of coffee and a Danish. I don't like to leave her, in case she wakes up."

"I'll be right back."

I took the elevator down and got coffee and pastry for both of us. It didn't bother me at all that I had missed

Amelia's confession. What difference did it make now? She was not Willard Platt's killer. I got on the elevator and went back up. Mrs. Benzinger smiled when she saw the food. I had to be firm about her not paying me.

I sat in the second chair and we opened the bags. The coffee was better than I expected and the pastry was just what I needed, something sweet to give me a lift.

"I'm sorry you missed her," Mrs. Benzinger said, obviously believing that Amelia had lapsed into a coma.

"I'm sorry she's in such distress. This must be very painful for you too."

"She's my only sister."

There was a sound and I looked toward the bed.

"Reen?" It was faint and breathy but it was Amelia.

"She's awake!" Maureen Benzinger got up and went to the bed. "Amelia? Did you have a good sleep, dear? Chris is here to see you."

I couldn't hear what the response was but Mrs. Benzinger turned and motioned me to the bedside. Amelia's eyes were open and she fixed them on me.

"Mrs. Chester? I'm Chris. You asked to see me."

"Chris." She moved her hand so it touched mine. "Chris. I want to tell you. About the gun. About Will." It was a struggle for her to put the words together.

"Yes. I'm listening."

"—shot Will."

"Who?" I asked. The first word had been little more than a puff of air.

"Harry," she said, pushing the word out. "Harry Franks . . . Harry . . . shot Will."

"Harry Franks shot Will," I repeated, stunned by the revelation.

"Harry. Yes. Harry." She closed her eyes.

"She's fallen asleep again," her sister said. "I don't think you'll get any more out of her today. She really exerted herself."

"She told me what she wanted to tell me."

"Did you understand her?"

"Yes I did." I looked back at the sleeping woman, then at my watch. It was time to go.

Downstairs, I called Jack.

"His best friend shot him?"

"That's what she said. I don't think we even talked about Harry on Saturday so she wouldn't know I'd ever heard of him. I'll have to talk to him, Jack, but I can't do it today. I don't have his address and I don't have the time. I think he lives in Manhattan, and that's quite a drive from here. What I want to know is whether he owns a car or has a license."

"I'll find out before I leave today. You don't honestly think he came out to Oakwood to settle a fifty-year-old score, do you?"

"No, but I have to check it out now that Amelia has told me her story."

"OK, honey. I've got my orders."

I drove back to Oakwood and went straight to Melanie's house without picking up Eddie.

When she opened the door, she said, "What happened to you? You look terrible."

"That's why I'm here. I need some tea and sympathy."

"I've got plenty of both. Come on in."

I almost collapsed when I got to her sofa. I had the feeling I had been running on pure momentum, and when I came to a stop, I was totally without energy. I sat and rested while Mel made the tea, nearly falling asleep in those few minutes. The whiff of tea brought me back.

"Tell me," Mel said. "I've never seen you like this."

I told her, consuming two cups of tea and more cake than I usually eat in a week. But as it went down and warmed me, it revived me. I finished the story of the hospital in the Bronx, in the room of the dying woman who had been Willard Platt's first wife.

"You don't really think this little old man came and stuck a knife in his friend on April Fools' Day, do you?"

"No. Jack is checking on whether he has a car or a license, just to cover all bases, but I don't think he had anything to do with it. I don't think this was a planned murder. I think it happened because Willard and the killer argued about something. No one would come from New York or anywhere else to kill Willard Platt with the victim's own cane."

"His wife could," Mel said. "She knew the cane would be there in the garage. She kills him with it, takes it in the house, brings it down to the basement, opens the window a crack, and goes upstairs to discover the body. It's the simplest solution."

"I don't believe it," I said.

"Neither do I. Have another piece of cake. Your color is coming back. I just don't see seventy-year-old women offing their husbands by pushing a knife into them. Does that make me politically incorrect?"

I laughed. "The son could have done it almost as

easily. He could have scooted around the front of the house and—"

"How would he know to go around the front?" Mel asked.

"Good question. Maybe he knew his mother always sat in the back. Or maybe he went around the garage, saw his mother through the window, and retraced his steps. But there's another possibility. He could have tossed the cane in his car and driven back when no one was home, like during the funeral."

"Which would explain why he wasn't at the funeral. Good point, Chris. And he has a key, so he goes inside, dumps the cane, and goes home. Was anyone in the house during the funeral?"

"I don't think so. I went back to the house with Willard's friend Harry when the service was over. We needed a key to get in."

"So who else is there?"

"Mr. Vitale, the nurseryman."

"Well, he had it easy," Mel said, as though she were a great expert on carrying out a homicide. "He could take the cane with him, maybe even hide it in the woods across the road from the Platts', and just shove it through the window when he saw everybody leaving the house. You said the Platts thought the window might have been open a crack."

"Yes. But why did he wait years to do this?"

"Maybe Willard made his life miserable in a million little ways that built up his anger. Maybe he reached the breaking point. Those things happen, you know. You should have seen what you looked like when you came in. You were on the verge of collapse. Maybe for Vitale it wasn't a physical thing so much as a mental one. Maybe Willard needled him about things. You never know."

I was almost laughing as I listened to her. She was concocting a great scenario for murder. "Maybe you're right. He certainly didn't tell me the whole truth about that land deal, assuming Roger did."

"So you've got two men with long-standing grievances against Willard Platt. The wife has the best opportunity, it seems to me. What's her motive?"

"Just living with a difficult man for almost fifty years."

"That'd do it for me," Mel said cheerily. "But I hope I wouldn't wait fifty years and I hope I wouldn't think that murder is a better solution than divorce."

"Maybe it's a generational difference," I said. "Anyway, I just can't see that nice, grandmotherly woman doing what was done to her husband. Thrusting a knife in someone's body cannot be an easy thing to do."

We sat quietly for a minute or two. "It was the hospital that did it to me," I said. "I'm not even sure that poor woman was alive when I left the room."

"It was brave of you to go to her, Chris. She's not a friend or a relative. I bet she was pleased you came."

"I only went for the information."

"But you went. How many people do you think visited her?"

There couldn't have been too many. Besides her sister, who else was nearby? I looked at my watch. "I'd better get Eddie. He's at Elsie's and it's been a long day for both of them. I just wanted to revive myself a little before picking him up." Mel walked me to the car and said the kind of nice things that she is famous for. I gave her a hug before I drove away.

* * *

The call came while we were eating dinner. It was Mrs. Benzinger to say that Amelia had passed away that afternoon. She wasn't sure exactly when but she was grateful that her sister had been able to say whatever it was she had told me.

I said a few phrases of condolence, surprised at how hard this death was affecting me. A few days ago I had never heard of this woman; today I had listened to a deathbed statement. I had the feeling she had kept herself going until I got there.

"Amelia?" Jack asked as I hung up.

I nodded. Eddie was at the table, and we would not talk about this till later.

Jack had the coffee made when I came down from putting Eddie to bed. He'd had a good time today, starting with nursery school where they had made something out of clay that he would bring home when it dried and got painted. Then Elsie had taken him for a walk and taught him the names of some trees. I read to him and he fell asleep.

"Your friend Harry Franks doesn't own a car and has no valid license," Jack said.

"I didn't think so. I called Winnie when I got home and she gave me his phone number and address. He lives on the West Side of Manhattan. I'm going to see him tomorrow."

Jack looked at me with a twinkle and some detective humor slipped into what he said. "You're not afraid he'll shoot you?"

"Honestly? No. I just want to know what it's all about."

"He's had a lot of time to polish up his story."

"Everybody in this case has. I think I'm most disappointed in Mr. Vitale. I was really on his side till Roger told me what Vitale had left out."

"What do you suppose Winnie Platt has left out?"

"A life full of annoyances. And still, the high school kids loved him. The drama teacher thought the world of him. I don't know, Jack."

Before nine I called Sister Joseph and told her what had happened with Amelia, which she found interesting, and also that I had talked to a neighbor about the accident.

"Keep at it," she said.

I promised I would.

21

Harry Franks lived in a prewar apartment house in the West Nineties between Broadway and West End Avenue. I had a terrible time finding a place to park, eventually sliding into a metered space on Broadway as a car pulled out. I fed the meter all it would take, which gave me an hour, and hoped I could conclude my conversation with Harry in that length of time.

He was expecting me and buzzed me into the lobby a second after I rang his bell. There were strange food smells in the hall and I wondered what ethnic background they represented. You could probably write a history of New York on the kitchen smells of its apartments.

Harry opened his door and ushered me in. It was a dark apartment and he didn't turn any lights on. The furniture had become shabby over the many years it had been in the living room. I imagined that when his wife died, the apartment simply froze. He would never change anything.

"So what can I do for you?" he said when we were sitting.

"Harry, you're not going to believe this, but I found Will's first wife."

"Amelia? No kidding. How'd you do that?"

I told him and he seemed impressed.

"Now refresh my memory," he said. "Why were you going to try to find her in the first place?"

"To find out who shot Willard Platt fifty years ago."

"Oh, yeah, right. He got shot. You talk to her?"

"I went to visit her last Saturday but she wouldn't tell me. Then I got a call that she was in the hospital and wanted to see me. I went there yesterday."

"She say anything?" He seemed eager for an answer.

"She said you shot Will."

"Nah. She got a bug in her head."

"Harry, I need to know the truth."

He looked away from me. I wasn't sure whether he had done it or if Amelia had named him just to clear herself. Maybe it wasn't a deathbed confession; maybe it was an old woman with a grudge putting the blame on an innocent man. Maybe, I thought, they had done it together.

"That Amelia," he said, still looking away. "What's she look like now? I bet she's still a beautiful woman, even if she's got a few gray hairs."

"No gray hairs that I could see, but she's a woman who takes care of herself."

"She always did. What a body that woman had. Will should've taken better care of her."

"What are you saying, Harry?"

"He married her for the wrong reasons. He didn't love her. He was in love with himself. He'd been in the war, he'd got out in one piece, he wanted a good time. He met this gorgeous girl and swept her off her feet. They do that anymore? Sweep a girl off her feet?"

I smiled. "I think it still happens, Harry."

"So they got married. Went down to City Hall with two witnesses and tied the knot. I gave them a bottle of champagne for a wedding present. The marriage didn't last much longer than the champagne."

"That's a lovely gift."

"They went away, they came back. Next thing I know, they can't stand each other."

I listened, hoping this was leading somewhere.

"He wasn't nice to her, you know? She didn't deserve how he treated her. She was a nice girl. I think she really loved him when she married him. She called me once or twice."

"When they were married?"

"Yeah. Said he got angry at her all the time. There wasn't anything she could do right. She cried."

"I guess she needed sympathy," I ventured.

"Well I gave her sympathy, all right. She deserved it. She needed it."

"And?"

"And things got worse. One night she called me." He stopped, looking pained. "She say anything about me when you talked to her?"

"Nothing. Just that you shot Will."

"It was a long time ago. I guess she doesn't remember."

"What happened the night she called?" I prompted.

He didn't seem to want to go on. "She said something about how Will said he couldn't stand living with her anymore. He wanted out. She said he had a couple of drinks and walked out on her. I was feeling really bad. I asked her if I should come over. She said sure, why not? So I went over to their apartment, went upstairs. She was alone. She said she didn't think Will was ever coming back, but I knew Will better than that. He'd left all his clothes there and he wore good clothes. I knew he'd come back for them."

"How long did you stay?" I asked.

"Oh, I don't remember. You're talkin' fifty years. A coupla hours, I guess. She broke out the good scotch and we drank a little."

I had a feeling *a little* meant *a lot*. "What happened?" I asked.

"You mean . . . ? Nothing happened. She cried. I patted her on the shoulder. I listened. That's what happened. Then Will came home."

I felt a chill. It was a perfect setup for violence, assuming at least one of the men was violent. "What happened?"

"What do you think happened? He was sore as a pup. He wanted to know how long this had been going on. I said nothing was going on. He didn't believe me. I could tell he'd been drinking, but so had we. It was just a bad scene. I could understand why he would think maybe there was something between Amelia and me, but I couldn't forgive him for the way he'd been treating her. Next thing I know, he's in the bedroom and he comes back with a gun and he points it at me."

"You must have been very frightened."

"Lemme tell you. Here's this guy I love with all my heart, who got me through the thick and thin of the war. He's had too much to drink and he's pointing a gun at me because he thinks I did something terrible that I didn't do. And he's bigger than me besides."

"What happened, Harry?"

"We had a fight. Amelia was crying and screaming, thinking one of us was gonna end up dead, which could've happened. And I'm scared to death I'm gonna be the dead man. I don't know how it happened. Maybe I wasn't as drunk as him, but somehow I got the gun away from him and in the excitement I pulled the trigger."

"And he got hit."

"Yeah. He got hit." He took a deep breath, as though he was glad he'd finally gotten it off his chest.

"And then?"

"Then Amelia called a girlfriend of hers who was a nurse and this nurse came over and took care of him. It wasn't a big deal, at least she said it wasn't. She fixed him up, bandaged him, told him to take it easy, and said none of us should ever talk about it or she'd lose her license. So I haven't talked about it for fifty years."

"Thank you, Harry."

"Boy, I can't believe I kept that a secret for so long."

"What I don't understand is how the two of you stayed friends."

"We *were* friends. We were like brothers almost. Will came over to see me a coupla days later like a dog with his tail between his legs. He couldn't apologize enough for accusing me and Amelia. He said he'd had a lot to drink and he couldn't really remember all that happened. But he was fine and he and Amelia were splitting up. He walked in with a cane, I remember, just a plain-lookin' thing in dark wood. While we were talking he pulled the top part out of the bottom part and showed me there was a blade inside. And he said something like, 'Don't ever pull a gun on me again, you hear?' As if I'd pulled a gun on him." He shook his head. "And that was it. We stayed friends. He moved out of the apartment when he felt better and he took all his clothes with him. In a coupla months he had a new girlfriend, and that one he married for good. Her name was Winnie."

"And you and Amelia?"

"She called me the next day, said how much she appreciated my saving her life, which I didn't do. And I never saw her again."

That surprised me. It had sounded like the beginning of a romance. "I see," I said noncommittally.

"I would have, but she didn't want to. I think she was lookin' for another big, good-lookin' guy like Will. I wasn't very big and I was never very good-lookin'."

"You're a very nice man, Harry," I said.

"Yeah." He grinned. "All the girls say that."

"So you and Will really stayed friends all those years." I still found it surprising.

"All those years, yeah. I went to his wedding with Winnie. That was some bash, I can tell you. And he came to mine. And we stayed friends. I can't tell you what it did to me when I got that call last week that he was dead. It was like a piece of me was gone. I kept remembering the war, how we got off the landing boat and made it through the water up onto the beach with the Japs shootin' at us as if we were devils. A coupla times there, if it hadn't been for Will, I wouldn't've made it."

"That's quite a story. You know, Will's children don't know anything about his first marriage."

"I been thinkin' about that. We never talked about it, you know. You think maybe Winnie doesn't know?"

"I think it's possible. I'm not going to tell her. I did tell Roger."

"Isn't that somethin'? He never told them. I guess it got to be like a dream that didn't work out."

"I guess so." I got up and put my coat on. My meter would be running out of time. "Will must've been a pretty tough guy."

"He was. Winnie's a good girl for putting up with him. But he was good to her, I gotta say that. He learned his lesson the first time."

"I guess he did. And he carried a cane the rest of his life. Maybe that was to remind him that he shouldn't lose control."

"Maybe so."

I was near the door and ready to leave when I remembered something. I turned back. "What became of the gun, Harry?"

"The gun, the goddamn gun. Well, I took it with me when I left their apartment. I wasn't gonna leave it around for him to pull on anyone else. I took a long walk that night, over to the Hudson River. There's a coupla places you can get right near the river on a walkway. I looked around to make sure no one was looking and I threw it in the water. It's probably still there, if anyone wants to go fishing for it."

I thought that was likely to be true, along with a hundred other heavier than water secrets. "Harry, I have to tell you something. Amelia was very ill when I saw her. Her sister called last night and said she died."

"No." He looked as though he had just been struck.

"I'm sorry. She was really very weak. She knew she didn't have much longer to live."

He got up from his chair. He wasn't a very tall man. We stood nearly eye-to-eye. Amelia had probably been taller than he. "Thanks for comin', Chris. It was nice to see you. I hope you figure out who killed Will. Someone should hang for it."

I wasn't sure I agreed with his assessment, but I promised I would do my best. When I got back to my car, the meter was just turning red.

I had left Eddie with Elsie, so I had time to spare. I drove back to Oakwood, made myself a quick lunch, and then drove over to the house Carolyn Haney had pointed to across Oakwood Avenue from hers. I rang the bell, hoping Fran Goldman would be home, and she was. I introduced myself to her, explained why I was there, and she invited me in.

"That must have happened five years ago," she said. "Why are you interested?"

"I'm looking for a motive for the murder of Willard Platt."

"The man who was killed on April Fools' Day?"

"That's the one."

"His wife was driving that car that crashed. What could that have to do with his murder?"

"Probably nothing, but I can't find a motive anywhere else."

"I've heard he was on bad terms with a lot of people."

"Like whom?"

"The mayor and council, his son."

"I've heard about those. Do you have any information about that?"

"No. It's just gossip. The women I carpool with were talking. He was a strange man, I think."

"I think you're right. But you know, he was very generous to the high school drama group."

"I didn't know that."

"He didn't talk about it, but I know he contributed time and money."

"I guess you never know about people."

Thinking about the story I had heard that morning, I had to agree. "Can you just go over with me what happened the day of the crash?"

"I was reading the paper. I heard the sound and knew something terrible had happened. I went to the living room window, but I could hardly see anything. It was winter and it got dark early. Also it was snowing. But I heard sounds, a woman's voice. A car door slammed a couple of times. I put my coat on and went out the front door. I could make out the car because the rear lights were on. And the headlight on the driver's side was beaming through the snow. The other headlight had gotten smashed, so there was only the one beam. I dashed back inside and called the police."

"So you're the one who called first."

"I think so. There wasn't enough time from when I heard the crash and picked up the phone for anyone else to have called, but it's possible. They got here pretty quick, at least, I heard the sirens a few seconds after I hung up. I don't know what else I can tell you."

"Did you go back outside to the car?"

"Yes. People were coming out of their houses. I saw Carolyn. The police wanted us out of the way so I went home."

"Did you see Mrs. Platt?"

"Yes. I heard later she had gone to Carolyn's to get help, but I think I got to the phone before she did."

"Did you see anyone come over who seemed to be a friend or a family member?"

"All I can tell you is that there were a lot of people there by the time the police came."

"Thanks, Fran."

I thought about it as I walked out to the car. There was nothing new, nothing that didn't corroborate what Carolyn had said. I signaled my turn at the corner of Oakwood Avenue, then changed my mind. Instead I changed the signal and went the other way, ending up at Doris Platt's house. There was still the question of the new will.

She was home and invited me in. We sat at the kitchen table and I refused her offers of tea and coffee. "Doris, what do you know about the will your father-in-law wrote?"

"I've never seen it. I know, because Winnie told Roger, that Roger was cut out of it. That didn't surprise either one of us, considering the relationship they had."

"It may not have been a surprise to Roger, but was he upset when he heard about it?"

"My recollection is that he was almost relieved. He said it gave him freedom. His father owed him nothing and he owed his father nothing. He said he had never wanted his father's money, that he would earn his own. And he has."

From the way she spoke, it was clear Winnie hadn't told her about the discovery of the new will. "I'd like to talk to Roger about that," I said.

"Oh dear."

"Is something wrong?"

"It's just that he was very unhappy about both of us discovering him last Saturday. The police have been bothering him, not at that apartment, but here. I don't know if he'll see you."

"Would you call and ask?"

She went to the phone and dialed. She kept her voice down while she spoke but I heard her say, "She's here now." There was some discussion, then she turned to me, still holding the phone. "Can you come here tonight about eight?"

"Sure."

The conversation ended and she hung up. "He's really in a mood. But he'll be here tonight."

"Are your children gone?"

"Yes. They left this morning."

"Did Roger stay here while they were here?"

"Overnight, yes."

So they were still keeping up appearances. "I'll see you at eight."

22

I arrived at the Platts' house about five to eight. Roger's car was in the driveway and he was the one who opened the door for me. He didn't respond to my greeting, just closed the door behind me and walked into the living room. I took my coat off and laid it over a chair. Doris didn't seem to be around, which unnerved me a little. I wanted her presence as a calming effect on her husband.

"What is it you want?" Roger asked when we were both seated.

"First of all, I want you to know I haven't said anything to your mother about your father's first marriage and I don't intend to."

"How did you come to know about it? You may have told me but I've forgotten."

"Your father's friend, Harry Franks, told me."

"Harry. Right. Did Harry come out for the funeral?"

"Yes, he did."

"I'll have to call him. OK. What's on the agenda?"

"Your father's will."

He said something under his breath that I was sure was unflattering. "This is not your business. This is the business of my family."

"You're right about that, but I probably know more right now than your family and the police know. I think if I can put it all together, I may be able to figure out who killed your father."

He seemed to consider this. I knew he didn't want to talk to me about anything; he had made that clear when I saw him on Saturday. But I wanted to watch his face when I told him about the new will. It was very quiet in the house. If Doris was there, she was making no noise. While I was glad to talk to Roger without her presence, I was uncomfortable knowing I was alone with the prime suspect in a homicide.

"Well, maybe you can," Roger said. "The police have pretty much homed in on me. I've talked to a lawyer and he doesn't think they have anything concrete against me—they can't; there isn't anything. I didn't kill my father."

"You said you had a difficult relationship with him."

"I had almost no relationship with him. I visited my parents because I love my mother and I couldn't deny her her grandchildren. You're aware that Doris and I live apart. No one else in the world knows that, not my parents, not my children, not even the place where I work. One great thing about communicating by e-mail is that the other party has no idea where the message is coming from. I could be across the country for all they know."

"What do you know about your father's will?" I asked.

"I've never seen it. I don't know where it is. I don't know the name of the lawyer he used. I know that after my father wrote it, my mother told me he had cut me out without giving me a cent. That's what I know about my father's will."

"What did that do to you, hearing that he had disinherited you?"

"It didn't do anything to me. I didn't want his money. When I was young, I wanted his approval. Maybe I even wanted his love. I didn't get either of those things. I never had any idea what my father was worth—I still don't. And it makes no difference to me. I'm sure there's enough there for my mother to live on. That's the only thing that matters. Where it goes after that is of no interest to me."

It was a grand statement, if true. The way he said it, it was very believable. "So your father never talked to you about his will."

"We hardly talked at all."

"Suppose I told you he wrote another will a few years ago."

He stared at me. "How do you know that?"

"Toni called me just before she left. They had suddenly thought about the will and your mother went to wherever it was kept and found both the old one and the new one."

"Why would he do that?" he said, looking bewildered. "All the grandchildren were mentioned. What did he change?"

"At your mother's death, you and your sister share equally." I watched his face. This was the moment I had come for.

"You're joking."

"I'm not."

"This is terrible," he said. "If the police find out—"

"I haven't told them. But they can find out very easily."

"My God, they'll think— You're sure about this?"

"I'm sure."

He rubbed his cheek with his palm. He was a nice-looking man, taller than his father, trim, his hair thinning. Right now he looked almost scared. "Why didn't my mother tell me?"

"She just found out last weekend. It was as big a surprise to her as it is to you. Can you think of any reason he would have done this?"

He shook his head. "It gives me a motive," he said. "Don't you see that? This is the concrete thing that my lawyer said they didn't have."

"Your father never told you he was doing this," I pressed.

"My father and I had very few conversations in the last ten years."

"Was your mother happy living with your father?" I asked.

"Reasonably. He was good to her, I'll say that. I was the one who wouldn't toe the mark." He seemed almost to be in a daze. If this was an act, he was a better actor than his father had ever been.

"Mr. Platt, I want to ask you about the land your father owned."

"I'm sorry. Did you say something? My mind is just wandering."

"The land on the hill that your father owned. The land Mr. Vitale was interested in buying."

"The land, yes. There are several acres, ten or twelve, I think. Vitale only asked for one or two, across the road from our house, the section that abuts the nursery."

"You said he might have been interested in building houses on it."

"I'm sure he was. I'm sure the reason he gave for wanting it was just a subterfuge. That area is zoned for residential buildings. He wouldn't even have needed a variance."

"Have there been other people interested in buying that land?"

"Oh, yes. Over the years builders would contact my father and ask if he was interested in selling off some of it."

"What do you think your mother will do with it?"

"I don't know. It's got to be worth two million or more. If she needs money, she may consider selling some of it. I don't really know what my father left to her. Since I wasn't going to inherit, I had no interest in that."

It sounded very convincing to me, that and his appearance. "Well, I would guess your mother is well off. If she decides to sell, she'll probably have a buyer very quickly."

"Lots of buyers. That's prime land. Look, I'm really very upset by what you've told me. Are we finished here?"

"I'm done." I put my coat on and dug my keys out of my bag.

"I'll have to talk to Mom about that new will. I can't believe—" He stopped very suddenly and I turned to look at him.

"Did you think of something?"

"I don't know. Maybe."

I waited, but he said nothing else. As I started for the door I heard a door open somewhere else. Then Doris, in her coat, came from the kitchen area.

"Chris, I'm glad I got back in time to see you."

I was about to say hello when Roger said, "Doris, did you ever hear that Dad made a new will?"

"No. Why?"

"Mom never said anything to you? Or Dad?"

"All I know about is that will he cut you out of."

"Absolutely crazy," Roger said.

I wished them both good night and went out. They hardly knew I was leaving. Roger was explaining to his wife what I had told him.

"What a family," Jack said. "You're pretty sure you surprised him with the news?"

"He was in a daze, Jack. He couldn't believe it."

"Well, his mother called you while you were out. You can call her back. It's not too late."

I could smell coffee and knew Jack had been waiting for my return to have his. It had become one of our nightly rituals and we both enjoyed it. I told him I wouldn't be long and dialed Winnie.

"Chris," she said. "Harry called me. He said you'd been to see him."

"Yes. I saw him this morning."

"He said it had to do with that bullet wound the Medical Examiner found in Will."

"Yes, we talked about that."

"It seems so funny. I was married to my husband for so many years and he never said a word about it. I always thought that was a little malformation or a childhood scar. I never asked."

"I think it didn't matter much to him," I said, not certain how much Harry had said.

"Actually, I called about something else. The police asked if my husband left a will."

My heart started pounding. "What did you do?"

"I told them I was looking for it. I'll have to get back to them. I've been thinking. This new will, while I'm glad to see my husband had a change of heart about Roger, this will makes it seem that Roger could have killed his father for the inheritance. I know the police consider him a suspect."

"They have no proof, Winnie."

"Well, you know, there are a lot of things. Roger has a key to the house, so he could have put the cane in the basement while the rest of us were out, like when we were at the funeral. He has no alibi for that time."

I smiled at the word alibi. "If he's innocent, he doesn't need an alibi."

"But who knows where he was or what he was doing that morning?"

"I think you're upsetting yourself, Winnie. I don't think Roger did it."

"Roger didn't do it," she said firmly. "He may not have gotten on well with his father, but he would never kill him. He's a good and decent person."

"I agree with you."

"So this is what I was thinking. If there were no second will, there would be no reason for Roger to kill his father."

I didn't like where this was going. "But there is a second will."

"Not if it disappears. Not if no one found it. The old will is perfectly good."

"Winnie—"

"You've never seen the second will, Chris. You don't know that it exists."

"It's true that I've never seen it."

"I think nobody has ever seen it," Winnie Platt said. "I think the only will Toni and I saw was the one I remember Will writing a long time ago. I have that one right here. I found it in the file drawer where Will told me he kept it. There's nothing else in the folder marked 'Wills.' "

"Wills?" I said, noticing the plural.

"Well, I have a will too, of course, in case I died first. I own half the house, there are some stocks in my name. The lawyer said I should have a will too."

"To whom did you leave your money?"

"To Will first, then to my children and grandchildren. Our wills were not the same. I remember the discussion we had in the lawyer's office."

"And that was the last one you wrote?"

"It's the only one I ever wrote. Surely if my husband had written a second one, I would have updated mine. Doesn't that sound reasonable?"

She was giving me the logic behind her decision. "All I can say is, your husband must have had a reason for changing his mind. I think that should be honored."

"I can't let my son be arrested for a murder he didn't commit." It was the most forceful I had ever heard her.

I really hate dishonesty. I don't mean that we should not tell the kinds of little white lies that spare people from pain and embarrassment. I mean everyone should try to tell the truth so that people will not get hurt or cheated, so that business and government and the rest of life can function smoothly.

But I am also a mother. I could feel inside me how Winnie felt. She knew her son was innocent, and she wanted to erase the only real evidence that might be used against him. I didn't blame her, but I couldn't go out on a limb and assist her.

"Winnie, I'm sure there's a copy of the new will at a lawyer's office." Not to mention the fact that I had already told Roger.

"You may be right." She spent a moment thinking about it. "I suppose it could surface someday. The lawyer could die and they could clean out his files. Or he might call here to ask a question."

"Those things are possible."

"But it might not happen for twenty years. The lawyer is in New York. I didn't put a notice in the *Times* when my husband died. I'm going to think about this, Chris. I hope you see my point of view. I'm a mother protecting her son. You have a son. You would do anything to protect him."

She was right about that. "Yes, I would."

"Any mother would. Well, it's quite late. I'm sure we'll talk again soon."

I hung up the phone feeling washed out.

"You off the phone?" Jack called.

"Yes."

"Let's have some coffee. You look a little weird."

"I feel weird."

Jack had cut up a pineapple and we each had a quarter. It was sweet and juicy with great aroma. I waited till I was halfway through the fruit and the coffee before telling him what Winnie had said and what Roger had told me earlier. I was concerned, not just about Winnie's ethics, but about my own. I had never been placed in a situation where I was asked to withhold material information. Not that Winnie had asked explicitly. I had marveled, while we were talking, at how she had intimated things without actually saying them. It was clear that she now regretted having told me about the second will. She was right that I had never seen it, never read a single word of it, but I had no doubt of its existence. It was even possible that as we sat here enjoying our dessert and coffee that the second will no longer existed. She could have put it in the fireplace, in one of the many fireplaces in that wonderful house, and burned it to ashes, along with the lawyer's card, so that no record of his name and address could be found. It had been drawn up by a different lawyer, Toni had told me, someone they were not familiar with.

What a strange turn of events. Who wouldn't be happy to find he was heir to a great deal of money? In this case it was a trick question. In this case, inheriting from your father might become a death sentence.

23

I got Eddie off to school on Thursday morning and, pencil in hand, sat down to do some thinking. Jack and I had had a long conversation last night about ethics, morals, and the law. We didn't agree about everything but we were both concerned about Winnie's decision to make the second will disappear. One of the many things that occurred to me was that if Roger had actually committed the murder and was found guilty of it, he wouldn't inherit from his father regardless of his father's wishes. But if he were innocent, he would be deprived of half his father's estate, which seemed to me to be fairly large. He had tossed off the price of the land, two million, as though he were talking in thousands, but I had no sense that the amount was inflated. I've seen the appraisal of the plot of land our house is on and I catch my breath at the number. The fact that Aunt Meg bought it for a few thousand dollars many years ago doesn't diminish its current value.

Until Winnie's call last night, I had begun to think that perhaps this homicide was over a land deal after all. And it might not be Mr. Vitale who had killed Willard Platt, although that was still a possibility; it could have been Winnie. Winnie was shrewd; I had seen that last night when she coaxed me obliquely not to talk about the second will. If I happened to be blind to the value of land, that didn't mean that a woman whose husband owned ten or twelve acres didn't know what it was worth. And maybe she and her husband disagreed on the disposition of the land. I was assuming that the Platts had a lot of money, but I didn't know that for a fact. Maybe they didn't. Maybe it was the land that was the bulk of their holdings. It was possible they had gone through whatever money they'd accumulated and Winnie wanted to sell the land and her husband didn't. Maybe they fought about it. I didn't really believe that Winnie went out to the garage with the intention of killing her husband, or even harming him, but from what I had learned about him, it was in character for him to blow up and be violent. And maybe that had happened on April Fools' Day. With Will gone and the land sold, Winnie would have enough to live on for the rest of her life.

Having made some vague notes in my book, I looked up the mayor's number and called him. His wife got him to the phone.

"Mrs. Brooks?"

"Good morning, Mayor Strong."

"You figure out who killed Willard Platt?"

"Not yet. I talked to Mr. Vitale after you and I spoke last week."

"Over at the nursery?"

"Yes. And I have some questions about the land on the hill."

"I'll try to answer them," he said, sounding cautious.

"Is that area zoned for residential use?"

"Exclusively, but we made an exception if the nursery

wanted to expand. And if the Vitales give up the nursery, which I think they will when they get a little older, that reverts to residential also. We're not gonna have a supermarket moving in at that location."

I was rather happy to hear that myself. "Are the lots zoned for any particular size?"

"Minimum one acre. You thinking of buying?"

"I don't think I can afford an acre up there. That's pretty pricey land, I hear."

"I wouldn't be surprised if it went for up to half a million an acre."

That was a lot more than Roger's estimate. "Are you aware of anyone wanting to buy that land from the Platts?"

"Willard Platt didn't take me into his confidence," the mayor said shortly.

"But I'm sure you know what's going on in town," I said, hoping to prod him into being more forthcoming.

"I know everything that goes on in Oakwood. And yes, there is interest in building on that land. I'd guess if Mrs. Platt put it up for sale, she could close a deal in twenty-four hours. That's prime land up there. I could give you the names of three builders who would drop everything to get their hands on it."

"Thank you, Mr. Mayor."

Prime land. I had the image of builders crouching at a starting gate, just waiting for the signal that would let them dash up to the Platts' and make an offer they couldn't refuse. Even if the mayor had exaggerated the value of the land, it would surely net Winnie several million, and with one acre zoning, no one would be very close to her house. Her privacy would be preserved and she would be able to live more than comfortably.

But there was another aspect to the value of the land, and that was Mr. Vitale. What if he had learned only recently what the current asking price was? From what he had said to me so candidly, he still felt a strong antipathy to Willard because of the land sale that hadn't happened. I had just discovered the value of the land a few minutes ago; maybe he learned of it in the last few weeks and the festering anger had become inflamed. If he owned that land now, he might be able to sell it at a huge profit, especially if he had built a house on it. What was good for Winnie made Vitale look more like a suspect. It would also account for the long time that may have elapsed between the land deal and Willard's murder.

I called Joseph and told her what had happened since our last conversation. There was a lot to report and she listened quietly.

"So it's possible that someone killed Mr. Platt in order to make an offer for the land to Mrs. Platt."

"Exactly. I'm pretty convinced that Willard didn't want to sell, but that doesn't mean Winnie didn't."

"But why would she want to sell, Chris?"

"For the money. I can't think of any other reason. I don't think it would be for the company."

"You'd think that Willard would have agreed to sell some of the land if he needed the money. He could have sold the land across the road or up the hill, leaving plenty of land around his house to preserve his privacy."

I could tell she wasn't convinced that my new motive was sound. "Maybe I'm grasping at straws."

"Not at all. The value of the land is startling. And then there's the will. I do hope Mrs. Platt doesn't do what she indicated she might."

"So do I."

"Tell me again what Roger said when you told him of its existence."

"He was shocked. He couldn't understand why this would have been done. But a little later something occurred to him."

"Did he share it with you?"

"No, he didn't. He seemed to light up as though he knew why his father had changed his mind. But he didn't give me an inkling of what it was about."

"But you've learned something, Chris. You've learned that there is a reason. Willard Platt felt he owed his son. What did his son do to make him feel that way?"

I had no idea. "Whatever it was, he didn't make an agreement with Roger. He just changed his will, knowing that Roger wouldn't find out about it till he died."

"Even if there wasn't an explicit agreement, Willard may have said something like, 'If you do this, I will make it worth your while.' And Roger may have done what was asked of him."

"Do you think it has something to do with Roger moving out of his house?"

"It might. That might be a jumping-off place for you. Find out when and why he left his wife."

"OK."

"Look at it this way, Chris. Mrs. Platt called you and told you obliquely that she intended to hide or destroy the second will. She didn't say, 'Keep quiet about it and I'll make it worth your while.' "

"Not at all."

"But if she came to you with a handsome present, you would have the feeling that it was a payoff."

"I certainly would. And I hope she doesn't."

"That may be what happened between father and son."

"I think I'll take a walk over to the Sound and sit and think."

"That seems like just the right thing to do. And you can hear the splash of the water and inhale that wonderful air."

"I'll let you know if it works," I promised.

It was the right thing to do. I took my notebook and a lightweight beach chair and set out for the cove. A group of local homeowners own it in common and pay to have it kept clean. It's very private, a crescent of beach on that section of the Atlantic Ocean that is called the Long Island Sound. Across the Sound from where we live is the north shore of Long Island. One of the things that will probably keep me here forever is this little piece of land and the lapping saltwater. I used to come here as a child when we visited Aunt Meg. Gene and I swam—or, more correctly, jumped the waves—while my good aunt sat with her mother's eyes riveted on the two of us. Many years later, when Jack and I were beginning the relationship that would end up as our marriage, we walked this beach in bare feet or sandals, talking about the things young lovers talk about, or not talking at all.

The beach is one of Eddie's favorite places. Although he's too small to do much besides wade in the shallow water, he loves the feel of it. Our serious swimming is done at the Oakwood pool, but that's a different thing altogether.

I opened my chair on the sand and sat so the sun was

not in my eyes. No one else was there. It was breezy, as it usually is near the water, but not too cold, and the sun was brilliant. I could feel its warmth, like a healing salve, through my jacket. I was sure it was making me healthy although what I really wanted was for something to make me more insightful, something to explode in my mind and give me answers.

What was I missing in this tragedy? I closed my eyes and started thinking about the marriage of Roger and Doris Platt. If there was something that Willard wanted from Roger, maybe it was to keep that marriage together. Perhaps Roger and Doris told Winnie and Willard that they were planning to separate, perhaps even to divorce, and the elder Platts prevailed upon them not to. That could have been the reason for Roger moving out but pretending to remain at home. In reality, they were separated, but to the world they were living together. Willard, pleased that his son had adhered to his wishes, changed his will.

That would certainly explain the facts as I knew them. What other explanation could there be? I got up and walked along the edge of the beach. I was wearing sneakers and I moved closer to the water, leaving footprints in the wet sand behind me.

The death of the child. Perhaps Roger wanted to sue his mother for the death and Willard convinced him not to do it. It wasn't unheard of to sue a friend or a relative in an accident case. I didn't think, from what I had heard, that Winnie would have suffered in any way from being sued; that is, any more than the loss of the grandchild caused her to suffer. Detective Joe Fox had made a point of saying that she was properly licensed, the car was registered and in good condition, and it appeared that the road conditions had caused an unavoidable accident.

But someone had mentioned to me that she was probably speeding. I thought about that. Probably speeding. But there were no witnesses to the accident. The women who lived on or near Oakwood Avenue had heard the crash, but had not seen it happen. They would have had to bring in experts to testify that the car was traveling at a speed unsafe in those conditions. Could Roger have intended to sue?

I bent over and ran my hands through the dry sand beside where I was walking. It felt warm to the touch. It was spring and my favorite months of the year were coming soon, when the trees leafed out and the spring flowers bloomed, when the air became so hot that you could hardly stand to wait to get into the water. And here I was thinking of a cold, snowy evening in winter.

Maybe Roger had hired a lawyer when his son was killed and the lawyer had suggested a civil suit that he had set aside at his father's bidding. Maybe that was what this was all about.

I didn't like it, not any part of it. There was nothing substantial. Everything was guesswork. Even finding that second will proved nothing. Yes, it gave Roger a motive. But Winnie hadn't known of the second will, I was sure of that, and Roger seemed stunned to learn of it.

Think about the land, Kix, I told myself. Maybe there was something in the Vitale deal. Roger was familiar with the terms of the sale, that was sure. Maybe it was Roger who'd had the foresight to include the clause forbidding Vitale to develop the land for residential use.

That would surely have pleased Willard, who might have seen it as a close call.

But where did that leave me? It gave a motive for the second will, but not for murder. The whole idea of the second will was very intriguing. It was the exact opposite of what one would expect. Usually, a new will is found cutting one of the heirs off. In a typical mystery, someone hears about a new will being written, denying an heir his inheritance. The heir then attempts to kill the benefactor before he can sign the new will, making the old one invalid.

Here everything was the reverse. No one knew about the new will until after the death of the benefactor. The person whose benefits were substantially reduced by it was Toni, the sister who lived halfway across the country, and she had not known of its existence until a week after her father's death.

I sat down on the chair, having made a full circle of the beach, took my sneakers off and shook out the sand. Then I put them back on and went home.

The phone rang almost immediately after I got inside. I picked it up and heard a man's voice say, "Mrs. Brooks?" and then, "This is Roger Platt. I don't know what game you're playing here, but I've spoken to my mother and she assures me there is no second will."

"I'm sorry to hear that," I said. I then told him about the call from his mother last night, after I had returned from talking to him.

"I don't believe you," he said angrily. "I think you made this entire story up to trick me into saying something that would make me appear to be a killer. But you can't trick me, Mrs. Brooks. I didn't kill my father."

"You don't have to believe me, Mr. Platt. Call your sister and ask her about the new will. She's the one who found it and called me to tell me about it."

"I'll just do that," he said, and hung up.

I had no idea whether Toni would tell him the truth. I had begun to wonder whether anyone I had talked to in this whole case had been honest. I wondered if maybe I should just stop thinking about it for a day or two and see if the police could make sense out of it.

24

When Eddie came home from nursery school, excited about all he had done that morning, we had lunch and then he went to sleep. About two in the afternoon the doorbell rang. I saw a police car in the driveway as I went to open the door and wondered whether someone had decided that maybe I was a suspect, since no one else had emerged as the killer.

Officer Malcolm stood at the door and asked if he might come in. We sat in the family room.

"I understand you wanted to talk to the officer first on the scene in the Platt accident a few years ago."

"That's right. I thought maybe there was a connection between that and the murder of Willard Platt."

"I hardly think so, Mrs. Brooks."

"Could you tell me what you remember?"

"Sure. I got a call on the radio that there had been an accident on Oakwood Avenue, and I was only a couple of blocks away, so I put my siren on and went there. I arrived before anyone else—all the cars came eventually—and the first thing I did was to see if anything could be done for the boy."

"He was still in the car."

"Yes, ma'am. The grandmother was out of the car. She'd gone to a nearby house to call for help, but someone else had phoned in before that. In fact, when I got there I think she wasn't back yet. The boy was in awful shape. He was really smashed up. I don't know if he was dead or alive, but I talked to him, just in case he could hear me. He was dead when they got him to the hospital. I called for an ambulance, but they'd already sent for one."

"Did anyone call for the boy's parents?"

"I didn't. I think one of the neighbors might have. I had a lot to do at the scene what with the terrible weather and cars coming. It was one of the worst nights of my life."

"I can imagine. Did the parents show up?"

"Oh boy." He looked as though he were trying to remember. "Maybe the mother, maybe not. They all went to the hospital because that's where the boy was. I really didn't see much of that."

"What about the grandmother?"

"I think she rode in the ambulance with the boy."

"Did you issue her a summons?"

"No, ma'am. In my judgment, it was road conditions that caused the accident, not her driving."

"What did she look like?" I asked. "How badly was she hurt?"

"Not bad. It was just the right side of the car that hit the tree. She escaped with almost nothing, a scratch maybe. But she was taking it very hard."

"I heard they needed the jaws of life to get the boy out of the car."

"I called for that right away, when I called for the ambulance. I could see he was pinned in there."

"So it took some time before they went to the hospital."

"That's right. But I'll tell you, they worked very quick. They really did their best."

"Did you have any reason to think that Mrs. Platt was speeding?"

"She said she wasn't, and I can't believe any right-minded person would have been going fast in that weather. She's not your typical kid in a sports car."

"Was the boy belted in?"

"I'm pretty sure he was. I think they cut the belt to get him out."

"What kind of investigation did you carry out?"

"Well, I didn't carry it out, ma'am. But I think they were pretty thorough. There was a death. They take that very seriously."

"And no one thought there might have been another car involved or a pedestrian trying to cross the road?"

"No evidence of that."

"Exactly when did that accident happen?"

"Five years ago this past February."

"I guess that's it then. Thank you very much for coming."

I watched him drive away. Joe Fox must have suggested he come to the house. I was grateful for it, but I hadn't learned anything new.

The phone rang a few minutes later, and when I answered, it was Toni Cutler. "Hi, Chris, how are you?" she said cheerily, and my guard went up.

"Just fine. Have a good flight home?" I am notoriously poor at small talk and consider it a waste of time.

"Oh, yes. Good to get back to the family. I hear you and Mom took a drive together."

"Yes, we did. She's doing fine. I think she'll have her confidence up very soon."

"I'm really relieved to hear that. If she can get herself around, she can be her usual independent self."

I wondered where all this was going. "Yes," I said, not wanting to prolong the agony.

"You know, I've been thinking. You were so extremely helpful to us, Chris. We want to do something to show our appreciation."

So there it was, the bribe to keep me quiet about the will. "I didn't do much, Toni, and I was happy to do it. I know you appreciated the little I dug up. I'm glad I could do something."

"No, no, really. Mom came up with a super idea. She'd like to make you a present of an acre of land on the hill."

I was stunned. People don't go around giving away half-million dollar presents, and they certainly don't give them to me. When I caught my breath I said, "Thank you, Toni. I couldn't accept it. It's very kind of your family, but believe me, I couldn't accept it under any circumstances. And we're very happy living where we are."

"You think about it," she said, still using the light tone of voice that contrasted with the more down-to-earth one I had heard when she was in Oakwood.

"As long as we're on the phone, can you tell me approximately when Mr. Vitale tried to buy the land from your father?"

"Let's see. It was quite a long time ago, nine or ten years at least. It could even have been longer."

I made a note on a scrap of paper on the counter. "And the date of the second will that you found last Saturday?"

There was a pause. Then she said, "There's no second will, Chris. I don't know what you're talking about."

So Winnie had gotten to her. "Did Roger call you today?"

"I talk to my brother all the time."

"Did you talk to him today?" I asked.

"He called, yes." The voice was coming back down to earth.

"It's really important that I know the date of the will."

"The original will—that is, the only will Dad left—was written a long time ago. Mom knows when. They didn't talk about it much except to say that their affairs were in order."

"And Roger didn't benefit."

"That's because of their relationship. We've told you all about that."

"It's the second will I'm interested in," I said. "I want to know whether it was written before or after the terrible accident."

"There's only one will and there's my doorbell. Got to go. Think about what I said. Mom really wants you to have that land." She hung up.

I didn't know whether to laugh or cry. I picked up the phone, called Jack and said, "You're not going to believe what the Platts just offered me."

Joseph had been right, as she usually is, in suggesting that I find out the dates that important events occurred, and that included the new will. I knew I couldn't ask Winnie, so it looked as though the only other person who might be able to tell me was Roger. Did he know? I wondered.

Had his sister effectively stifled all discussion of the will by convincing him that it didn't exist?

When Eddie got up, we had our afternoon snack and then got in the car. There was a chance Roger might be home, working there instead of at his office. He wouldn't be happy to see me, but the only other way I could reach him was to go through Doris, and she had seemed pretty reluctant the last time I asked.

"Who are we visiting?" Eddie asked as we went inside the building.

"A man named Mr. Platt."

"Is he Mrs. Platt's boy?"

"Yes he is. He's her son, but he's a grown man."

We went up to the third floor and down the hall. I rang the bell and waited. There was noise inside, someone coming toward the door.

"Who's there?"

"Chris Brooks."

He pulled the door open, ready to say something, but stopped himself when he saw Eddie. "Come in. You can only stay a minute. I'm working and I can't take much time away from it."

"I have only one question. Do you know the date of the second will?"

He shook his head. "This is getting very involved and unpleasant. I owe you an apology."

"Don't bother. I know what it's about." But the fact that he said it meant that he had extracted the truth from his sister. He knew there was a second will.

"I asked Toni that very same question. She didn't have the exact date, but it was several months after my son—after the accident. But for the record, there isn't any second will and never was. That's the way my mother wants it."

I ignored the last statement. "What favor did you do to earn half your father's estate?"

"I don't want to discuss this with you."

"Were you intending to sue for the loss of your son?"

"It crossed my mind, but I never took the first step. It was too—my gut wouldn't let me. How do you put a price on your child?" He looked toward Eddie, who was quietly going through a magazine on a coffee table.

"I don't know," I said, feeling tearful. "I couldn't. But I know it's done."

"Well I didn't do it."

"When did you leave your wife?"

"Around that time. Everything just piled up and it became too much for me."

We were standing there in his living room, facing each other a few feet apart, two strangers linked by a murder and all the detritus that had surfaced in its wake. He had to know what the key was, and if he didn't tell me, no one else would. Toni and Winnie had locked the gate. It was the family against the rest of the world. "You still see your wife, don't you?"

"Yes. I have nothing against her. I just don't seem able to live with anyone anymore, not since my boy died. I need to be alone. I need to be responsible for only one person." He sat down in the nearest chair, as though he no longer had the strength to stand. The conversation was enervating him. "And I couldn't live in that house anymore with my son gone. He was the most wonderful child, smart, loving, good-natured. He was the child I tried to be for my father when I was young except I never did anything right. How could he have thought that money would make a difference to me?" He looked up.

"He didn't know you," I said softly.

"That's the truth. He never tried. All I ever wanted from him was his love and approval, and they were the two things he didn't give me—couldn't give me, because he didn't love me and didn't approve of me. I was an April Fools' Day joke to him. That's when I was born, did you know? And when he was murdered, I was out having a drink with a friend to celebrate."

"Then you have an alibi," I said.

"Probably not. I think we actually got started a little later in the day. I even turned my cell phone off so I could enjoy the moment."

Which was why his wife hadn't been able to reach him. "I see."

"You know, my life is easier now with my father gone. If I want to see my mother, I can just go over there. I don't have to ask whether it'll inconvenience him or annoy him. I'm glad he's gone. He was a thorn in my side and it's been pulled now and the wound is mending. If you think I'm confessing to something, I'm not. I'm just being honest. My life is easier and I'm glad he's gone."

"Thank you."

"Do you intend to tell the police about the second will?"

"Not unless I'm asked, and I can't see that they'll ask me."

"Did you ever see it?"

"No. Toni called and told me about it."

"Well . . ." He stood. "Thanks." He held out his hand and we shook.

"Come on, Eddie," I said.

"No. I wanna look at the pictures."

"We have magazines at home. Let's go."

He waited a moment, looking at a double-page spread of a red car, then came over to me. I said goodbye and we left.

25

Driving home I wondered if I cared anymore who had killed Willard Platt. Roger had suffered enough in his life, most recently because of the death of his son. I could understand his feelings, his urge to get out of the house after that death. The boy had been a young teenager. He would have made noise, laughed, talked, argued, played music. The absence of the sound must have been chilling. The emptiness for the parents must have been unbearable. I looked in the car mirror and checked my little boy, looking out the window as we neared home. I could not imagine my life without him, with the knowledge that this young life had ended. And for Roger Platt there were all those other emotions stemming from his relationship with his father.

What a strange man Willard Platt had been. I remembered the day at Prince's when Eddie nearly ran him down with the cart and I had seen the cane lying on the floor. He had no murderous enemies, hadn't had them for decades. He didn't need to carry a concealed weapon to protect himself. He used a cane because it set him apart from other people, called attention to himself, perhaps made people act deferentially toward him. That was what he wanted, deference, something his son had never given him.

I have often wondered where anger comes from. There are people who seem to respond to situations with anger when evenhandedness would be more appropriate and accomplish more. Among the nuns I have known at St. Stephen's, there have been women with such good hearts, women who would help you before they were asked. Yet I never wondered why they were so good, as I now wondered why someone like Willard Platt was filled with so much anger. The woman who had stopped to talk to me at Prince's had said he was famous for suing people. It wasn't a reputation I would want for myself. Perhaps it padded his ego, made him feel powerful. And yet this same man lay down on the grass in front of his house and waited for teams of high school students to locate him so they could share in a treasure hunt.

A strange man. And now his wife and his daughter, and his son too, it appeared, had been drawn into a deception that even I was marginally involved in. I felt deeply conflicted. I possessed information, the existence of which I could not prove, but which was material to a homicide. If I told the police what I knew, they might arrest Roger and they would surely give Winnie a hard time. If I kept it to myself, I had my conscience to live with. But if the second will no longer existed, if the police could not find it and Winnie denied its existence, how could it have any effect on the case?

I could not believe that Roger had killed his father. I thought it more likely that Winnie had. Here it was her son's birthday, and her husband, instead of doing something nice for their son, was playing games with other people's children. Maybe she sat in the sunny windowed room at the back of her beautiful home and thought about it, stewed about it, eventually exploded with anger over it. It occurred to me that she might actually have heard my cries and the banging on the front door and refused to answer for her own reasons, but the frantic sounds could have started her thinking about how badly her husband had treated their son. What if I hadn't driven up the hill that afternoon? Would Willard Platt still be alive?

At home, Eddie jumped down onto the driveway and ran to the back door. I followed more slowly. I had a feeling I had accumulated all the information about this case that I was likely to find, and I still had nothing convincing. Somewhere in that collection of information had to be the answer or answers that would finger a killer.

We went inside and I started cooking dinner, handing Eddie small pieces of raw vegetables to eat with his apple juice. I did all my tasks automatically, my mind trying to sift through the facts, the events, to find the thing that was wrong or the thing that should have rung a bell.

What if Harry had lied to me about the ownership of the gun? Suppose it was Harry's, not Willard's. Where did that leave me? Nowhere, I thought. It made little difference whose gun it had been. What if he had kept it for half a century, not tossed it in the river? I shrugged as I peeled potatoes. It made no difference. All I had learned from that story was that there was a reason Willard Platt began to carry a cane, even a reason why he carried canes that were weapons. It didn't give me a clue to his killer.

Amelia was gone and she hadn't killed Willard. I didn't think Harry had either. Vitale was still a good suspect, a man simmering with hatred for many years.

And how could Winnie have thought she could buy me off with a gift of land? Did I come across as the kind of person who would lie for money? That troubled me. I put down my scraper, pulled out a kitchen chair and sat down, leaning my face in my hands. Let's think about this, Kix, I instructed myself silently. Suppose you and Jack had the money to build a house on a piece of property worth almost half a million dollars. Would you have been more receptive to the bribe? OK, don't call it a bribe; call it an offer. Might you have said you wanted to think about it rather than turning it down immediately?

How can anyone know what one would do if circumstances were different? I believed—I wanted to believe—that whenever such an offer came to me, whatever the circumstances of my life, I would have turned it down as quickly and firmly as I had done today.

"Mommy?"

I looked up, almost surprised to see my little son in front of me. "What, sweetheart?" I said.

"Are you crying?"

He had seen me with my face down in my hands, so deep in thought I had not been aware of where I was. I felt terrible. "Oh no, Eddie." I scooped him up and set him on my lap, my arms around him. "I was just thinking about something."

"I thought you were crying."

"No." I stroked his hair, curly like his father's. "I'm very happy, honey. I have nothing to cry about." I kissed his forehead, gave him a squeeze, and held him in my arms. I had scared him and wished I were able to undo the last few minutes. "Everything's fine. Daddy's coming home soon and we'll have a good dinner together."

He hopped off my lap. "Can I have a pretzel?"

"Sure." I got him one and took one for myself. They were long rods and we crunched them together and he giggled. I patted his head and went back to making dinner.

26

"You're telling me this woman, this Toni something who's the Platts' daughter, called you from Chicago or wherever she lives and offered you an acre of prime land that could be worth half a million dollars just because you've been so nice to Mom."

"That's exactly what I'm telling you." Eddie was off to bed and we were sitting in our accustomed places in the family room, sipping our coffee and talking about what we had waited hours to discuss.

"And when you questioned her about the second will, the will she called to tell you about the other night, she said it didn't exist."

"You've got it. And her mother had told her brother, when he called her, that there was no second will. He was very annoyed with me for making up a false story."

"But the sister set him straight."

"Apparently. He had the good grace to apologize to me for the accusation."

"This is quite a family," Jack said. "They're better organized than organized criminals."

"Jack, I've been mulling this over all day. Stewing about it is more accurate. I know something that I can't prove about a document that has probably been destroyed by now. Its existence would make Roger Platt the prime suspect in his father's killing."

"You don't think he did it."

"Except for the fact that it happened on his birthday, which does change things, I have to admit. People get very sensitive on important dates, their birthdays, their anniversaries, the days that people who mattered to them died. If I didn't feel so sorry for him, the discovery of the new will and the fact that the murder happened on Roger's birthday might tilt me toward him. But it's all speculation, as I've been saying over and over. Frankly, I think I've come around to your position, that Winnie did it but she wants me to think Roger did to spare herself."

"You think she planned it for a long time?"

"She kept her license up-to-date."

"And we have only her daughter's word for it that her hearing is bad."

"True." I hadn't thought of that. I had considered everything Toni told me to be true since she wasn't a suspect. But the deafness in one ear was a very convenient explanation for Winnie's behavior, or lack of it, when I banged on her front door.

"I'll tell you how I see it; what the mayor told you about the value of the land, Vitale looks good to me for this."

"I thought the same thing."

"He's right there, he hops across the road and up the hill. Maybe something new happened recently that we don't know about between him and Platt and he boiled over, especially if he found out what that land is worth."

"But we're going around in circles, Jack. We have

three good suspects but nothing convincing on any one of them. I think I should let this rest, let my mind take a breather. It's making me dizzy, going around in circles. All I can see is second wills, canes, a knife in the back that isn't a knife."

"Then let it rest. Maybe the police'll figure something out. They do, you know." He gave me a sly smile.

"I know. And I appreciate their hard work. Imagine if Toni had called them before she called me about the will. The Platts could never have gotten away with retracting their statement."

"The cops would've been at their door in five minutes to read it."

"But they were too smart to call the cops. I think Toni called me before she and her mother had thought through the implications of the new will. In the end, they didn't want me knowing it either. I wish I knew the lawyer who drew it up for Willard."

"Lotta lawyers in this country."

And probably most of them in commuting distance of New York. "I'm taking the day off tomorrow," I announced. "I am taking my son for new shoes, which he badly needs. I'm going to call Mel to come over after she finishes teaching and we can talk about spring planting and town politics and forget this ever happened."

"Sounds like the right thing to do. Mind if I hit the books?"

"Not at all. How're you doing?"

"I'm getting there, but it'll take time. Some things have changed since I was on the street. I'm in a maze of laws and ordinances. Nothing that pertains to the Platt homicide unfortunately. Wish I could pull something out of a hat."

So did I, but I'm not that kind of dreamer. We finished our coffee and he took a pad of paper and a couple of books out and started reading while I went through the parts of the *Times* I hadn't read yet. Maybe a penitent killer would call and confess. But if he did, I hoped he would call the police station, not my number. Their credibility was a lot greater than mine.

As I had promised, I took Eddie for shoes on Friday morning. I had heard mothers complain about the cost of children's shoes before I was in a situation where it made an impression on me. Now it did. My pediatrician suggested what kind of shoes Eddie needed, and I did what he told me, gulping at the price and telling myself my son's well-being did not have a price tag. But when the salesman asked if he could show me a pair of sneakers for myself, I looked down at the worn canvas on my feet and said, "Oh, I think these are good for another season," suppressing the doubt I had that they would make it through the summer months. It's not that we are poor; it's that big purchases still make me quiver.

Eddie loved the shoes. He thought they looked just like Daddy's and I told him they did. He practically pranced out of the store as I followed with a bag containing the old ones.

"Where do you want to go now?" I asked when we were out on the street.

"I wanna see Daddy."

"We can't do that, honey. He's working in New York and that's a long drive. He'll be home for dinner."

"I wanna see Mel."

"Mel's teaching. She'll be home when school is over. She's coming to visit with Sari and Noah, how's that?"

"OK."

"Let's go see if we can get our new tree planted this weekend."

We drove up to the nursery and Mr. Vitale came to talk to me. "I think we can do it Saturday," he said, looking at a schedule. "The ground's warmed up in the last couple of weeks."

"Someone will be home whenever you come."

"Fine. You find out anything about the Platt murder?"

"I've turned over a lot of rocks but no killer has crawled out yet. I'm giving it up for a while. Nothing leads anywhere. Someone told me the Platts own about ten acres up there." I nodded up the hill.

"About that."

"The mayor said it's worth close to half a million dollars an acre."

"That's an exaggeration," Vitale said. "If it were worth that, I'd close the nursery tomorrow and sell the land. I could do better putting the money in a CD and living off the income than working my head off seven days a week."

"How many acres do you have here?"

"About seven, give or take. Want to look at your tree?"

"Sure. Come on, Eddie, let's look at our new tree."

We went down the slope and found it and once again I fell in love with it. The shape was so perfect, the branches so beautifully curved, like a small umbrella waiting to grow into a large one. All around us trees and shrubs displayed buds that were nearly ready to open. This was really my time of year.

"That's my tree," Eddie said, pointing to it.

"Well, let's see what grows faster, young man, you or that tree," Mr. Vitale said.

"I'm growing up." Eddie stretched his hands high to make his point.

"You may do it, son. That little tree's going to get bigger, but I'll bet you hit six feet before it hits three. See you Saturday, Mrs. Brooks."

And as always I found it hard to believe that a man who could be nice to a child could have committed a murder. "Thank you," I said as he walked away.

"You like the tree, honey?" I said to Eddie.

"It's a nice tree. It's a baby tree."

"Yes it is. It won't grow very big, but it'll have beautiful leaves and it'll grow this way." I showed him an approximate width with my hands. "Ready to go?"

"OK."

What Mr. Vitale had said about the price of the land rang true. He certainly didn't work at a nine-to-five job five days a week. He was open seven days a week in spring, summer, and fall, and I was sure his work was physically demanding. It made sense that if he could realize the kind of money those seven acres would bring at almost half a million per, he might consider living on the income. My work netted me very little, although I loved it, but after twenty-five years or so of back-breaking work, a man might understandably look for an easier life.

So maybe the mayor's estimate had been high—Roger thought it might be—and Mr. Vitale wasn't as potentially wealthy as I had thought. Nor would an extra acre of land have made a substantial difference in his life. Ask enough questions and the answers will drive you crazy.

* * *

I spent Eddie's nap time correcting papers from my class. Some semesters you get a class of great students; this was not one of them. I had a few shining lights but the rest were having a hard time staying awake. Having decided that the fault might well be mine, I had asked to be relieved of this class and assigned to a composition class in the fall. There would be more work, but it would be different and I was afraid of stagnating.

I had a lot of the work done by the time Eddie woke up. I gave him a snack and put water in my kettle, ready to boil when Mel and the children arrived. I even took my beautiful silver tea strainer, a wedding present from Joseph, out of its box.

Eddie stood in the front window, waiting for his company as though he hadn't seen them for years. I was reaching for a plate to put cookies on when he called, "I see them!"

"OK, I'll open the door." I put my platter on the counter and unlocked the front door, pulling it open to let the fresh spring air come in.

Sari and Noah saw me and started running. Mel waved and took off after them. We were all feeling pretty good and it was mostly the weather that was responsible.

"Good to see you," Mel said as they came inside. "Isn't it great out?"

"I love it. I've got the tea on. Want to sit out back?"

"How 'bout it, kids? Outside or inside?"

They all shrieked something and we decided outside had won. I found my one and only tray, loaded it, and carried it out the back door. The kids found toys in the garage and started to make happy noises while we sat at the table and I poured tea through the strainer.

"You're so elegant," Mel said.

"Me!" I laughed. "Wrong adjective. Look at these sneakers, Mel. I'm afraid I'll be arrested as a vagrant if I wear them out of the area."

"Sneakers don't count. But that's some tea strainer. Just looking at it makes me feel coddled. How's the Platt murder going?"

"It isn't. I've learned so many dirty secrets about that family and their friends, I can't believe there's any more, but I couldn't put my finger on the killer if my life depended on it."

"Something'll turn up," Mel said with the certainty of one who has no involvement whatever.

"I suppose so. I'm taking today off from thinking about it. And by the way, we're getting our little Japanese maple tomorrow."

"Where are you planting it?"

"Out front. It's too beautiful to hide here in the back."

"I agree." She inhaled the tea, then drank some. "Lovely. Mm."

"You have any idea what that land up the hill from the nursery would cost?"

"I thought you were taking a rest."

"Just asking."

"A lot, but I couldn't put a number on it."

"Half a million an acre?"

"Sounds high to me."

"That's what Mr. Vitale said. He said if it were that much, he'd close up the nursery tomorrow and sell the land and live off the income."

"So would I. I would make Hal work half time but I would teach because I love it."

"So would I," I said. "There's just something about teaching. I guess I feel about it the way Arnold feels about law."

"And Jack?"

"I don't know. I think he enjoys it, but he may want to do something else with it than what he's doing right now."

"There's time. We're still considered young." She laughed. "By our parents, anyway."

We drank more tea and talked some more and then Mel gathered her kids and walked home. I put the dishes on the tray and carried it all inside. Jack would be home soon and there was a table to set and a little cooking to do.

Everything was ready when I heard Jack's car pull up the drive.

"Daddy's home," Eddie called from the family room where he was waiting eagerly.

"OK," I called back. I dried my hands on a paper towel and heard the car door slam. I started for the back door. Then I heard it slam again.

I stopped, bits of information whirling in my head. The door opened and Jack came in. Eddie dashed to him, showing off his new shoes.

"Fantastic," Jack said. "They look just like mine. They're terrific. Gimme a hug."

That done, I got my kiss. "What's up?" Jack said, looking at my face, which must have indicated some of what was going on inside.

"Why did you close the car door twice?"

"I didn't. I got out and closed the front door. Then I got my briefcase and tie out of the back and closed that door. Why? Did I make too much noise?"

"No. You didn't make enough. I think I know what happened, Jack. I think I see it. It was right there all the time."

"The Platt case?"

"Uh-huh. It wasn't the way we all pictured it was. I think I know who did it."

27

I refused to talk about it while Eddie was with us, but I felt light and springy as we ate and I got him ready for bed. There was a motive now and a reason for the second will. Just the way it had always been in the past, the pieces were falling into place and unexplained happenings were starting to make sense.

"OK, tell me," Jack said as I came downstairs. "You've cracked this case because I took my briefcase out of the back of the car?"

"I have to check a couple of things but yes, I think I've got it. Hold on. I want to make a phone call." I got the local phone book, a skinny thing put out by one of the service organizations in town, and looked up Goldman. There were a few, but only one on Oakwood Avenue. I dialed and a woman answered. "Is this Fran Goldman?" I asked.

"Yes it is."

"This is Chris Brooks. I was over the other day talking to you about the terrible accident that happened a few years ago."

"Oh, sure. Hi, Chris."

"Fran, you said something that has been bothering me.

You said that after you heard the crash, you heard a car door slam a couple of times."

"I think that's right."

"Not once, a couple of times. Is that what you heard?"

"Yes. I remember that."

"Did you tell the police that?"

"I don't remember. Why?"

"It might be significant. It didn't bother you that it slammed twice?"

"I don't know if I thought about it. If I did, I suppose I assumed Mrs. Platt tried to get her grandson out and couldn't so she closed the door on his side."

But that side of the car had been smashed and twisted. They had needed the jaws of life to extricate the child. From the condition of the passenger side, she could never have opened the door. "Thank you," I said. "I just wanted to make sure that was what you heard."

Jack poured our coffee as I hung up. "Sounds like you're on to something," he said. "You've got a witness that heard a car door slam twice after the accident?"

"Yes. And it couldn't have been Winnie trying to get the boy out of the car because that door wouldn't have opened in the first place."

"So someone else got out of the car."

"Willard Platt," I said. "I think Willard was driving and Winnie lied for him."

"Keep going. Why did she lie?"

"Because maybe he was speeding and he was afraid of losing his license. If Winnie lost hers, it wasn't so bad; he could still take her shopping. But if he lost his, he lost his freedom. I think something was going on there. I have to talk to Roger."

"Finish your coffee. You can't go to a killer's house by yourself, and we don't have a sitter."

"He didn't do it, Jack. He just kept it under his hat."

"And his father gave him half his estate for keeping his mouth shut."

"I think so." I was ticking off points in my head.

"You look like you're solving one of the world's great puzzles."

"I am." I put my cup down and Jack went for seconds. I had to do this right or I'd never get a confession. They were all protecting each other.

"Another cookie?"

"Huh?"

"Oh Chris, you are really out of it."

"Thanks, honey. Yes, I'll have another cookie."

"He really loves those shoes."

"He wanted to go to your office to show them to you."

"I'll take him in someday. He should see where his daddy works."

"We'll both go. I've never been there either."

Jack actually works in an office these days, not in a precinct, as he did when I met him and until he passed the bar. He's in police headquarters now at One Police Plaza in Manhattan. His job is to review situations of police activity that might result in legal action. He has to determine whether cops may have used too much force, or may have acted illegally in other ways. It's a desk job but it uses the new knowledge that he has acquired in law school. Although I suppose there isn't much to see, I thought it would be nice for Eddie and me to make a visit.

I looked at my watch. It was still early enough to pop

in on someone, but I didn't rush through my coffee and cookie. When I was done, I told Jack where I was going. He looked troubled but I assured him I trusted Roger.

"Take my car," he said. "It's in the driveway."

I stood outside Roger Platt's door. Inside there were male voices and I hesitated. He must have a friend over. I couldn't decipher any of the conversation and finally I pushed the bell.

Roger Platt opened the door and said, "Come in."

In the living room was a young man who stood when I entered.

"This is my son Todd. Todd, Mrs. Brooks."

We shook hands and Roger said, "I thought my children should know what was going on in my family. Todd's in for the weekend and my daughter's coming in next Friday."

"That sounds good," I said. "I need to talk to you. It might be better if we talked alone. It won't take long."

"I'll go in the other room," Todd said. "I haven't checked my e-mail yet and I'm expecting some messages. Nice meeting you, Mrs. Brooks."

I waited till he was gone and the door had closed. "Mr. Platt, your father was driving the car that killed your son."

Roger Platt's eyes closed and he blew out a lot of air. "That's not true," he said. "Who told you this fairy tale?"

"Mr. Platt, I'm sure your family decided a long time ago to present a united front on your story, but it's a fiction, and I know it." I had to make him think I had some evidence so he would tell me the truth.

His eyes met mine. He looked miserable. Finally he said, "You're right."

"How did you find out?"

"I don't even remember. That whole period was like a fog. Maybe my mother told me when she was sedated. Maybe I figured it out myself."

"Why the deception?"

"He wasn't wearing his glasses. He'd had a drink. He wasn't a heavy drinker. He just liked a glass of scotch and water in the late afternoon."

"Why was he driving?"

"Because he knew better than anyone in the world. He didn't trust my mother at the wheel in that weather, so he said he'd drive. That's what she told me. They went outside to the car—her car—and she got in behind him so my son could sit next to him when they picked him up. After he'd started down the hill, Mom noticed he wasn't wearing his glasses and he said not to worry, he could see fine. Maybe he could and maybe he couldn't but his license said he had to wear them. He'd just had a strong drink and if he took a Breathalyzer test, the alcohol would show up. When the cops came, they'd smell it on his breath. And without his glasses— It was a split-second decision. The car hit the tree, he got out and walked home and she stayed and took the responsibility. I knew about it almost from the first day. I didn't know what to do. I hated having my mother blamed for the accident but if I said anything, there's no telling what would have happened to my father. He'd lose his license for sure. There was a chance he'd go to jail for vehicular homicide. Mom said to keep quiet."

"Did you talk to your father about it?"

"I did. He said he was sorry but that the accident hadn't been his fault." Roger looked over at me. "What else could he say? That he'd been drunk and blind and he killed my son because of it?"

"So you told him you'd keep quiet."

"Yes. He said he'd make it worth my while. That was the phrase. 'I'll make it worth your while, Roger. Just don't say anything.' He never did, of course, and I didn't care. There was nothing he could do to pay me back. Eric was gone, my life was—" He opened his hands, palms up. "And then you told me about the second will."

"And you knew that was how he had made it worth your while."

"I made that assumption, yes. It wasn't anything I had given much thought to. He was the same person after the accident as before, maybe a little warmer to me, I don't know. I never imagined he had changed his will. I mean, when you told me, it was like the most absurd thing I'd ever heard."

"And then you remembered."

"And then I remembered. That was how he made it worth my while to keep quiet about who had been at the wheel when my son died."

"Thank you, Mr. Platt. I hope we don't have to talk about these things again." I got up and went to the door.

"How did you know?" he called after me.

"Someone heard a car door close twice, well, not one car door as it turns out. She heard two car doors close and I guessed that there was another person in the car, your father."

"A little sound like that," he said.

"Have a good weekend with your son." I let myself out.

* * *

I stopped at a drugstore and called Jack to let him know I was alive and on my way to Winnie's.

"Stay away from that cane collection," he said.

"I will."

"And make sure Mrs. Platt stays away."

I turned up the hill, Jack's more powerful car taking it with greater ease than my own little one. The nursery was dark except for a light in the checkout area. The trees and shrubs were graceful silhouettes in the dark. I reached Winnie's and turned into the driveway. The garage door was closed and there were some lights on around the house, all on the first floor. She was downstairs reading or watching television.

I got out and walked over to the front door where, almost two weeks ago, I had banged and called to get her attention. Now I pressed the bell and heard a brief melody of chimes. Would she hear it or would she be sitting as Toni had described, her bad ear to the front of the house?

"Who's there?" her voice called tensely from inside, not too close to the door, far enough back that she could feel safe.

"Winnie? It's Chris Brooks. I'd like to talk to you."

"Go away. There's nothing to talk about."

"It won't take long, I promise. I've just been talking to Roger and I need to clear something up with you."

No answer and no sound. I wondered if she had simply gone back to her retreat in the big room she liked to sit in. "Winnie?" I called.

Nothing.

I stood there for several seconds, trying to discern any

sound from inside. Then I turned to leave. Behind me the front door opened.

"Come in," Winnie said.

I walked past her and she shut and bolted the door. Then we went into the living room and she turned some lights on.

"Where did you see Roger?" she asked almost accusingly. "I called and Doris said he wasn't home."

Oh, dear, I thought. I said the wrong thing. Roger might tell his children about his strange living arrangements, but I was sure he didn't want his mother to know. "I guess I caught him when he was coming in." I looked at my watch pointedly. "He wouldn't be there now. He said he was going out."

"All this running around. Why don't they sit down for an hour? Why are they always going somewhere?" She said it more to herself than to me.

"Winnie," I said, "I know you weren't driving the car the night of the accident."

She stared at me. "Roger told you that?"

"No, he didn't. I told Roger."

"How would you know such a thing?"

"There was a witness."

"There were no witnesses," she said. *"There were no witnesses."*

"Your husband wasn't wearing his glasses."

"You're making this up." She looked agitated.

"I'm telling you what I know to be true. I just want you to fill in the details."

"There are no details," she said wearily. "It happened. My grandson died. He was taken from us. If I'd been sitting in the front seat, it would have been me. I wish it had."

I wondered if she was aware she had confessed. "You were sitting behind your husband?"

She put her head in her hands and I thought of Eddie asking me if I were crying. Winnie wasn't crying, she was just tired of it all. She had lost two people very dear to her and she was alone in a big house with money to burn and nothing she wanted to spend it on. She was a bereaved woman who couldn't locate her son when she called. "I was in the backseat," she said slowly. "I was sitting behind my husband."

"And he wasn't wearing his glasses."

"No. We ran out of the house too fast. He forgot to put them on."

"He was driving your car?"

"Yes. It was in the driveway, waiting for me. He hated that car. It was too small, he said. It wasn't heavy enough. He always talked about how you needed a heavy car for protection. I just wanted a car that would get me around." She looked up to face me, her skin pale, her eyes hollow. "Maybe if the car had been heavy, Eric would still be alive."

"What did your husband do when he got out of the car?"

"He just stood there looking dazed. He'd had a drink before we left the house and I could smell the alcohol on his breath. Our little angel was sitting all smashed in the front seat and we just got out of the car unhurt. I said, 'It's my car, Will, and you're not wearing your glasses. You go home and I'll say I was driving.' That was it. He took off for home, walking along Oakwood Avenue in the snow. I ran to a house and rang the bell. The woman there called the police but I think someone else called first because when I got outside I could hear sirens. That's what happened."

"When did you see him again?"

"I called him from the hospital. He drove over in his car. He was wearing his glasses." Her eyes filled. "I told the police I was driving. It didn't matter. Eric was gone. They couldn't save him."

"Did you tell anyone the truth, that your husband had been driving?"

"Roger guessed. I didn't tell him at first, but Roger sensed it."

"Was your husband driving too fast?"

She didn't answer.

"Does Toni know?" I asked.

"I don't know who knows. Roger said he wouldn't tell. The police were very nice to me. There were no charges. I was a grandmother taking her grandson home and the car skidded. I had a clean record and I kept my car in good shape. It was better the way we did it."

"And your husband wrote a second will leaving half his estate to Roger to thank him for keeping the truth hidden."

"There is no second will," Winnie said.

There was no use pursuing that. "The day your husband was killed, that was your son's birthday, wasn't it?"

She nodded. "It was Roger's birthday. I asked Will if we could take him and his family out to dinner that night, but he didn't want to. He said the drama group had something planned and he didn't know how long it would take. We could have done it, couldn't we? The treasure hunt didn't take all day. It was over in the afternoon. He just didn't like spending time with Roger. There was nothing I could do about it. They were two men who didn't get along. It's very sad."

"It is sad, Winnie," I said.

"April Fools' Day," she said reflectively. "Will made a joke about it. He said his son had been an April Fools' joke on him." I recalled Roger saying very much the same thing to me. "I went into the hospital the night of March thirty-first when my labor started. I was excited and happy. In those days you didn't know whether it would be a boy or a girl the way they all know today. He was born about two in the morning. I wasn't thinking about the date. I was just glad he was healthy. When things started to go wrong between him and his father, I wondered if all our lives might have been different if he'd been born a few hours earlier, when it was still March. Will wouldn't have had anything to joke about, as though someone had played a trick on him. Do you think things would have been different?" She looked over toward me.

"I don't think so, Winnie. I think it was a matter of personalities, not timing."

"I suppose you're right," she said tiredly. She stood up as though every muscle in her body ached. "It's late. I think you should go."

She was right. Jack would be nervous, and I didn't want the police showing up because my husband was unable to leave the house to look for me. I got up and picked my bag up off the floor. In a bucket nearby, part of the cane collection stood. I walked over to look at them.

"Don't touch the canes," Winnie said sternly.

"What?"

"Don't touch them. Please. Just keep your hands off them."

"Sure," I said, wondering what was bothering her. "Thank you, Winnie. Good night." I went to the door and walked outside before she could catch up with me.

"So?" Jack said. "You got it aced?"

"Almost. I think I can do it tomorrow. I might want to call Joe Fox. Think I could rouse him on a Saturday?"

"If he's home, sure. Just leave a message that you've cleared the case. He'll call you back in ten seconds."

I smiled. "It's all very unhappy, Jack. Everybody's a loser."

"Except you."

"I'm certainly not a winner. I just put it together. It was Joseph who said I should look into the accident more carefully. I wonder if she suspected that Willard was driving."

"Sure she did."

The cups and saucers had disappeared while I was gone. I sat down next to Jack and rested against him. His books and notes were on the coffee table. He put his arm around me and I felt warm and safe.

"Winnie told me to stay away from the canes. She sounded very authoritarian."

"Maybe she was afraid you'd use one on her."

"I'm a real menace," I said with a laugh.

"Let's turn in. It's been a long day."

28

I woke up on Saturday knowing I had to do something difficult and unpleasant and I had to do it well. It was two weeks to the day since Willard Platt had been murdered, and today I had to elicit a confession or give it all up. I knew all that there was to know, all that was relevant. The police might have more information, especially technical stuff like fingerprints and DNA evidence, but they hadn't made an arrest because they didn't have enough, and I was pretty sure they were looking at the wrong suspect.

Outside, the spring-blooming trees made Pine Brook Road a rainbow of pink and purple, with a touch of white. The forsythia were fading, their green leaves replacing the yellow blossoms. If ever it was good to be alive, it was on a day like this. Rain was forecast for tonight, rain that we needed, but the day would be sunny.

I reminded Jack that someone from Vitale's nursery would be around to plant our new tree, so we couldn't both go out at the same time. That was all right with him.

"You going somewhere?" he asked.

"Eventually."

"I thought you said something about calling Joe Fox."

"I'm still thinking about it."

We had breakfast together, and Jack took Eddie out for a while and I stayed home. I was sorry I hadn't asked whether they would come in the morning or afternoon, but it was too late now. They had their schedule made up and were probably out on the truck at their first appointment. An hour wouldn't make much difference anyway.

When Jack came back, we talked about where we should have the new tree planted. I wanted to be able to see it from the living room window and I wanted it clearly visible from the street. We walked around on the front lawn and finally decided on a spot.

"What about the sun?" Jack asked. "All we've thought about is seeing it."

"There'll be sun. The front of the house faces east. Or sort of east. It's very bright in the morning."

As I finished speaking I saw one of the Vitale trucks coming down Pine Brook Road. Two young men got out in front of our house and started unloading our little tree. We showed them the spot we had chosen and they agreed it was a good place for it.

We moved away and watched them as they started digging up the lawn. Eddie asked a lot of questions, and Jack and the men answered them. I went inside the house and called Joe Fox's number, which Jack had written down in our address book.

He was there and came to the phone. I explained what I wanted to do.

"You think you've got this doped out?"

"I'm pretty sure, but you never know."

"I'll come with you."

"That won't be necessary. None of the people in this

case is violent. There was a motive and there was anger, but it was all directed against the victim."

"You sound very sure of yourself."

"I am."

"At least give me the address."

"I'll leave it for Jack. I just wanted you to know that I hope to have a confession later today, and if I don't, I'm giving myself a vacation from this case. I don't think anyone will ever turn up any hard evidence."

"Just a confession," he said.

"Just a confession. And a lot of circumstantial evidence that could probably be used against several people."

"Don't get yourself hurt."

"Thank you. I'll be careful."

I left a note for Jack with several addresses. I wasn't sure which one I wanted to start with. If I did it right, I might not have to talk to all of them.

I left things for lunch in case I didn't get back in time. Then I told Jack more or less where I was going and got in the car.

The driveway beside Roger Platt's house was empty and the garage doors were closed. Not sure whether anyone was at home, I went up to the front door and rang the bell. A moment later Todd Platt opened the door.

"Mrs. Brooks," he said with surprise.

"Hi, Todd. Is your mother home?"

Doris appeared at that moment, wearing a brown pantsuit with a pale yellow blouse showing at the neck. A gold circle pin was on her lapel. I wondered if I was interrupting something.

"Chris," she said. "Come in. It's nice to see you. Have you met my son?"

"Yes, I have. Do you have a few minutes?"

"Sure."

"I'll disappear," Todd said knowingly. "Can I take the car, Mom? I want to see if Rick's home."

"Go ahead. Got your license in your wallet?"

"Uh-huh." He grinned and rolled his eyes at me.

I smiled back. Mothers will always be mothers.

He pulled his keys out of his pocket and headed for the kitchen. Doris suggested the living room and we went there. For the first time I noticed the mantel over the fireplace. There were several family pictures there, all of them including a boy who must have been Eric, the lost child.

"He seems like a fine young man," I said, speaking of Todd.

"Thank you. He's in for the weekend. Roger decided to tell him about our living arrangements. I'm not sure it's such a good idea, but that's what he wants to do. Todd seems to be taking it pretty well, but you never know what goes on inside a person."

"I know that." It seemed an apt point of departure for me. "I wanted to ask you something, Doris. About the accident, if you feel you can talk about it."

"Go on."

"Did you know it was Willard who was driving the car that night?"

She pressed her lips together and looked down at her hands. "Not at first," she said. "At first I believed what I was told, that it was Winnie. How do you know about this?"

"A witness told me."

"Someone saw the accident?"

"Not exactly. But she heard something that led me to

believe Willard was in the car. Your husband acknowledged that it was true."

"We were never supposed to talk about it."

"When did you find out?"

"That whole period is so hazy. I was under a doctor's care for a while. I don't remember when I was told, but it was after a while, a few weeks or months after it happened. I was told not to say anything and I did what I was told."

"Did Roger tell you that his father promised to make it worth his while if he kept quiet about it?"

She looked at me as though she were just figuring things out. "The second will," she said slowly.

I didn't answer.

"They made a deal?" she said disbelievingly.

"I don't think they made a deal. I think your father-in-law asked Roger to keep quiet about it and promised vaguely to reward him in some way."

"I didn't know. This is the first I ever heard about it. I guess the rumors must have been true."

"What rumors?"

"That Willard was speeding. That he'd been drinking."

"I heard he'd had a drink," I said.

"Maybe more than one. Depended on the hour. He wouldn't let Winnie drive because the weather was bad. If she'd been driving, my son would still be alive. Winnie was a plodding driver. When I sat next to her I always felt like saying 'Giddyap' to make her go faster."

I'd had the same reaction myself when I accompanied her in the car the other morning. I decided the moment had come. "Why did you wait so long to kill him, Doris?"

There was no reaction. She looked as calm as she had

before I asked the question. "I didn't go there to kill him," she said, and I knew I would learn the truth.

"It was Roger's birthday," I prompted.

"Yes. It was my husband's birthday, the husband I loved and couldn't live with anymore because he was collapsing under the weight of his grief. Not to mention the hatred of his father. His father treated him like a nothing, but Roger's children loved him and Eric loved him the most. Eric was born on Roger's birthday, did you know that?"

"No," I said, feeling a terrible chill.

"Roger considered that a gift. They used to celebrate together, the two of them. There was something so special between them. Willard never made fun of Eric's birthday. He reserved that for Roger. He was a terrible person, Chris. I don't care how philanthropic he was. I don't care how many starving children in Africa his donations saved. He had a duty at home that he never fulfilled."

"You said you didn't go there to kill him."

"I didn't. I got up that morning and I knew it was my husband's birthday and my son's birthday. My husband didn't want to share it with me, and my son was more than five years gone. I wanted to do something to heal the rift. I knew Willard had a reputation for working with the high school kids. I thought, Why can't he see that his own son needs him the way those young strangers do?

"I thought about it all day. Winnie had said maybe the four of us would go out to dinner, but the invitation never came and I knew it was because Willard had said no. She didn't have the heart to tell me so directly. I drove over to see if I could talk to him, if I could be a peacemaker on that most important day. He'd always liked me. We'd always gotten along. I thought it was worth a try."

I watched her as she spoke. Her face was very somber and her eyes were somewhere else, perhaps looking at an event that had happened two weeks ago.

"Will was working on something in the garage. The door was open and I saw him as I pulled into the driveway. I might have parked on the road but I saw that the red flag was up for the mailman and I didn't want to block his access to the mailbox.

"I got out of the car and Will turned around and saw me. I said hello and he kind of nodded and stopped working at whatever he was doing. He had the hood of his car open. He took good care of his car. He took good care of things that were important to him.

"I said, 'Will, you know what day this is,' and the smile left his face. I said, 'You're a father, Will. You have such a good son. Couldn't you manage somehow to get back together with him? It would mean so much to everyone in the family.' " Her eyes were tearing as she recalled the painful conversation. "I promise you," she said to me, "I spoke in a conciliatory way. I didn't threaten him; I pleaded with him. It didn't do any good. He said something like, 'What do you know of my relationship with my son?' I almost laughed at that. 'I've been his wife for almost a quarter century, Will,' I told him. 'Of course I know. How could I not know?' "

I watched her almost reenact the dialogue. Her voice told the whole story.

"He became angry, nasty. He said the problem wasn't with him, it was with Roger. I listened to this man who had never given his son a fair hearing telling me how Roger had failed him. What he wanted was for Roger to come to him and beg forgiveness for his sins. He didn't put it in those exact words, but that was what he was saying. I think if Roger had decided to do that, if he could have demeaned himself the way his father wanted him to, they might have been able to renew their relationship, but on what terms? Roger would have spent the rest of his life walking on eggshells, wondering every time he opened his mouth whether he was saying the right thing, whether he might accidentally be offending his father. There was no way, and I knew it at that moment. All the anger I had suppressed for all the years that I knew Will came to the surface. I said, 'You're a nasty, mean old man. You have a wonderful son and you can't acknowledge it.' "

"That couldn't have gone over very well," I said.

"It didn't. It enraged him. And you know what enraged him the most?" She smiled. "It was the word 'old.' He said, 'You bet I'm nasty. You bet I'm mean. I live in a world where you can't let people take advantage of you.' It was 'old' that got to him. He couldn't acknowledge that he was old, and maybe he wasn't. Maybe I just threw that in to be nasty myself. I said, 'It's your loss, Will. I feel sorry for you.' That got him even madder. He picked up the cane and swung it at me, shouting at me to get out, to leave him alone. He hit me with the cane and I grabbed it, the bottom of it, hoping to pull him over, hoping to hurt him just a little for what he had done to his son. As I held it, he unscrewed the top, and when the two parts separated, I kind of fell backward because I was still holding the bottom of the cane so tightly I looked at him and he was standing there triumphantly, holding the curved top of the cane, a long knife protruding from it, pointing it at me. I was terrified. I thought he would kill me. It was one thing to whack me with the cane, but here he was pointing a dangerous weapon at me."

"I can understand how you felt," I said.

"Can you? Here was a man filled with hate coming after me with what looked like a sword. I took my half of the cane in both my hands, as if it were a baseball bat or a golf club, and I ran toward him till the cane pushed into his chest. He went backward, dropping the cane handle, and I grabbed for it and launched at him again, this time with the knife aiming for his chest. I was so angry, I was so furious. It wasn't just Roger anymore. It was Eric. That man killed my son, Chris. It was his fault. He was at the wheel with liquor in his system and his glasses on the kitchen counter. If Winnie had been driving, Eric would be alive. I felt it all through me and I just plunged that blade into him again and again. I didn't know how many times till I heard the report from the Medical Examiner."

Four times, I thought. She had run at him four times. "Then what did you do?"

"Will was bleeding and I was shaking, just absolutely shaking. I grabbed up the other half of the cane, tossed both pieces in the back of my car, and backed out of the driveway. As I got to the curb I saw the red flag up on the mailbox and I got out and put it down, hoping if there wasn't any mail, the mailman would just drive on and not look in the garage. Then I went home." She seemed exhausted. She breathed deeply a few times and wiped at her eyes. "I didn't know if Will was dead or alive and I couldn't call or Winnie would know I was responsible. I took the pieces of the cane into the house, wiped them off to remove my fingerprints, screwed them back together, and stuck them under my bed. I thought it was safe enough there until I decided what to do with it."

"What did you do?" I asked.

"I had the key to Winnie's house."

"You had a key too?" I had never thought to ask. I knew Roger had one but he had moved out.

"Roger gave it to me years ago, in case one of his parents had an emergency and I couldn't reach him. I waited till I knew Toni was taking Winnie out and then I drove over, let myself in, and left the cane in the basement room where they found it. The window was already open, so I just made it seem it had been thrown inside. I actually got up on a stool and stood near the window and pushed it in the right direction. Then I left. I didn't know when they'd find it, but I knew I wasn't going down to that basement till someone had seen it. I wasn't going to be the one who found it."

"Did you tell anyone you'd done it?"

"No one. I came home that day, two weeks ago this afternoon, and you know what? I felt light. I felt as if all my cares had been taken away. For a while I wondered if that was what it felt like to be on drugs."

"I think you should turn yourself in, Doris."

"I know I should."

"You can get a lawyer first if you want."

"Yes."

"Will you do that?"

She thought for a moment. "Yes, I will. I'll call our lawyer now." She got up and went to the kitchen.

I followed and stood where I couldn't see her but I could hear. She dialed and then had a brief conversation, telling the lawyer she needed to see him right away and would he come over? When she hung up, I said goodbye and went out the front door.

29

There were two cars across the street from the house. One was Jack's and he was at the wheel. The other I didn't recognize, but as I crossed the street, Joe Fox got out of it.

"Get a confession?"

"I think someone will be turning himself in at the police station," I said, using the grammatically correct form of the pronoun that did not disclose the gender of the unknown person.

"That's all you'll tell me?"

"That's all. I don't think you should question anyone till a lawyer arrives."

"They already call a lawyer?"

"They did," I said, smiling.

Jack had joined us. "You're not talking?"

"Not at the moment. You know, it's lunchtime. Why don't we all go out and have a nice lunch? It's over and I'm really hungry."

"I think I'll just wait till the lawyer arrives," Detective Fox said.

I didn't want to leave him alone, afraid he might ring the doorbell before the lawyer arrived. It wasn't that I didn't trust him. I just wanted to make sure that Doris had representation.

About ten minutes later a car pulled into the driveway and a man in casual clothes got out and hurried to the front door. Doris opened it quickly and the man went inside.

"It's all yours," I said.

"The killer gonna turn himself in?" Joe Fox said.

"That's the plan. If he doesn't I'll give you a name. Lunch?"

He seemed to think about it. "I'll just wait," he said. "I'm a detective. Waiting is the name of the game."

Jack took me up on the lunch idea and we went to the diner, to Eddie's delight, and had a good lunch.

"So why didn't I think of Doris?" he asked.

"Because everything pointed to Roger or Winnie. Or even Mr. Vitale. And plunging a knife into someone's chest doesn't strike us as a woman's crime."

"You said it."

"But I thought about Harry's story, how Will had pulled a gun when he found Amelia and Harry together. Harry tried to protect himself and Will got himself shot by accident. This was the same kind of thing. I could see Will using his cane to intimidate someone who angered him. After all, that was the reason he always carried one. And if someone got it away from him, as Harry had gotten control of that gun fifty years ago, that would be the beginning of the end for Willard."

"So she went to the house to be a peacemaker."

"That's what she said, and I believe her. It was a very

important day in all their lives, and she thought she could make Willard see the light."

"But she couldn't and he got sore at her for trying. Any hard evidence around?"

"She tossed the cane in the back of her car. Maybe there's some blood on the upholstery. That's pretty hard."

"Sure is."

"I think Doris was trying to get Roger to come back home. That's what it was all about. And he may have been thinking about it."

"Won't happen now."

"We don't know. She was defending herself against a very angry armed man. She didn't go there with a weapon. She used one that the victim used against her."

"Maybe you should get a law degree."

I reached over to where Eddie was sitting and moved his glass of milk so it wouldn't tip. "You've said that before. I don't think so."

"So Vitale had nothing to do with all this."

"Nothing at all. Not that he didn't have a motive. Eddie, be careful."

"I want some ice cream."

"Well—"

"Good idea," Jack said. "Let's all get some ice cream. Any objections?"

I valued my life too much to say anything.

"So what about the second will?" Jack asked after he had ordered our desserts.

"I have an idea. I think Winnie didn't destroy it. But I can't be sure. I expect with Doris confessing to this, Winnie will be happy to have the will reappear."

"This is a very sad case," my husband said.

"It is. I hope she can convince a jury the way she convinced me."

"You think she was telling the truth?"

"I do. She wanted her husband back, she wanted to get rid of the secrets in their lives. It just couldn't happen. Willard had a personality defect, if you will. He needed to lord it over his son. As you said, it's very sad. Even if Doris is acquitted, or better yet, if no charges are filed against her—"

"Unlikely."

"Right. That family is forever destroyed. A child gone. It breaks my heart. Oh Eddie, look what's coming."

His eyes were as wide as his smile. "Ice cream!"

"You bet. I can't wait to dig in."

Nor could he.

Our little tree had been planted on the front lawn and I saw it when we got back. It looked delicate and lovely on a background of grass that was now greening up. The men who planted it suggested to Jack that we think about enlarging the planting site with a few low-growing shrubs, and we talked about it and decided to do it.

Eddie, stuffed from our lunch out, went up for a nap, and I took the opportunity to drive up to Winnie's house. She opened the door, her face tearful, and let me in.

"You've heard," I said.

"Doris called me before she went to the police station I couldn't believe it."

"She didn't mean to kill him," I said.

"I know that. I know what was going on inside her. It was going on inside me too, but Will wouldn't listen to me. I tried to talk to him many times. I suppose I could have saved him that day if I'd heard them out in the garage, but I didn't hear anything."

"You thought Roger did it, didn't you?"

"I don't know what I thought."

I walked over to the bucket of canes in the living room and took one out. "Do you mind if I open this?" I asked, not waiting for her reply. She mumbled something as I pressed a button on the top of a beautiful silver-topped walking stick. As I pulled out the sharp knife within, I saw a curled piece of paper in the empty bottom.

"Chris—"

I ignored her and pulled that out too. It was page seven of a legal document. "You hid the pages in the canes," I said.

"Just in case you found a killer that wasn't my son. And you did."

"I'm glad you didn't destroy it. Roger deserves whatever his father left."

"He'll get it," Winnie said, "but not for a while. I'm still a young, healthy woman."

I smiled. "I'm glad to hear it. I feel the same way about you."

"Thank you," Winnie said.

"You're very welcome."

30

A lot of things did and didn't happen over the next several months. Doris was charged with a lesser degree of manslaughter, and I felt confident she would be acquitted or get a suspended sentence. Roger took a long trip and came back to try to live with his wife. Winnie offered me an acre of land near her house and I turned her down very firmly.

The Saturday after Doris's confession, I came down to breakfast to find a large box tied with pink ribbon. "This better not be a belated April Fool's Day prank," I said suspiciously.

"Open it," Jack directed.

Inside was a cordless phone for the kitchen. I was thrilled. It goes to the family room and all the way out to the backyard. If ever I decide to be a lady of leisure, it will help.

After the summer months were over, Mr. Vitale sold his land to a builder. He got over two million for the acreage and kept one acre for himself. They intend to break ground next spring. Before he closed down, we had him plant some wonderful shrubs near our red Japanese maple, which is the most beautiful tree on the street.

Willard Platt's second will was filed not long after Doris confessed to the killing. It had a bequest to leave a nice sum to the high school to be used for a modern, state-of-the-art auditorium, which they will build next year. It will be named the Willard Platt Theater, and they are planning a festive opening ceremony to which the whole town is invited.

I don't think I will attend.

Don't miss any of the
Christine Bennett mysteries

by Lee Harris

THE GOOD FRIDAY MURDER
The first Christine Bennett mystery

THE YOM KIPPUR MURDER

THE CHRISTENING DAY MURDER

THE ST. PATRICK'S DAY MURDER

THE CHRISTMAS NIGHT MURDER

THE THANKSGIVING DAY MURDER

THE PASSOVER MURDER

THE VALENTINE'S DAY MURDER

THE NEW YEAR'S EVE MURDER

THE LABOR DAY MURDER

THE FATHER'S DAY MURDER

THE MOTHER'S DAY MURDER

THE HAPPY BIRTHDAY MURDER

Published by Ballantine Books.
Available at your local bookstore.

Ballantine mysteries are on the Web!

Read about your favorite Ballantine authors and upcoming books in our electronic newsletter MURDER ON THE INTERNET, at
www.randomhouse.com/BB/MOTI

Including:

- What's new in the stores
- Previews of upcoming books for the next four months
- In-depth interviews with mystery authors and publishing insiders
- Calendars of signings and readings for Ballantine mystery authors
- Profiles of mystery authors
- Mystery quizzes and contest

To subscribe to MURDER ON THE INTERNET, please send an e-mail to
join-mystery@list.randomhouse.com
with "subscribe" as the body of the message. (Don't use the quotes.) You will receive the next issue as soon as it's available.

Find out more about whodunit! For sample chapters from current and upcoming Ballantine mysteries, visit us at
www.randomhouse.com/BB/mystery